HOLIDAY!

Alison Everitt

WARNER BOOKS

A *Warner* book

First published in Great Britain in 1995
by Warner Books

Copyright © Alison Everitt 1995

The moral right of the author has been asserted.

A CIP catalogue record for this book
is available from the British Library

ISBN 0 7515 1425 X

Typeset by M Rules
Printed in England by Clays Ltd, St Ives plc.

Warner Books
A Division of
Little, Brown and Company (UK)
Brettenham House
Lancaster Place
London WC2E 7EN

Dedicated to those of us to whom the Bahamas is but a distant dream and a floor-length sarong a must; to anyone who has ever carved their name on a sun-lounger, had to put on their suncream in the apartment to avoid being seen sitting up...but most of all to anyone who has secretly wanted to get the holiday Reps by their gaudy company scarves and *strangle* them!

Alison Everitt is a cartoonist, writer and broadcaster with a mind for expensive trips in the Maldives but a wallet for caravan holidays in her driveway.

This book is based on every package holiday she's ever begrudgingly had to pay for. Just about everything in this book has happened on or near her sunlounger, there are a couple of fibs and only a handful of artistic embellishments. Before you ask, yes, the Family From Hell does exist, and if you've never met one you're either:

a) extremely lucky
b) extremely rich
c) living in a world of your own
d) you *are* one
or...they're waiting for you on your next holiday.

Alison lives in North London and this is her sixth book.

Also by Alison Everitt:

The Condom Book for Girls
That's Fashion
The Modern Girl's Book of Torture
A User's Guide to Men
Oh No . . . It's Christmas!

Buy lots of these and you need never fear that she's writing the sequel on the sunlounger next to you...because she'll be in a villa in the Bahamas!

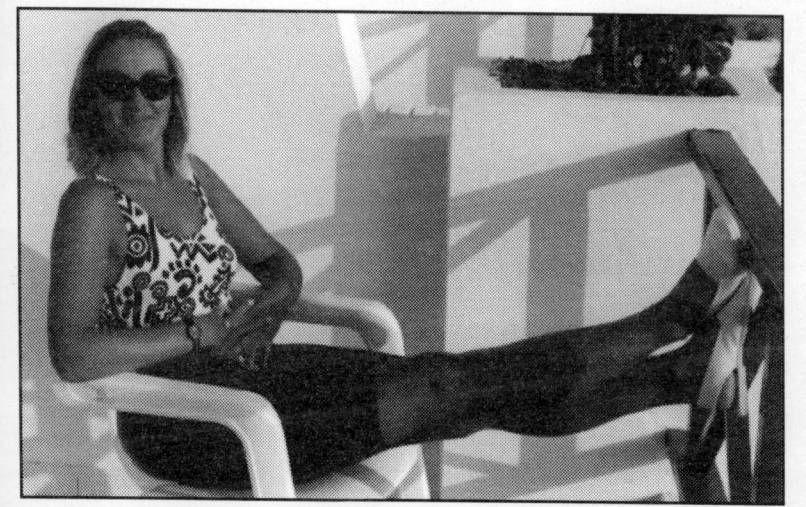

Contents

Introduction

If you're going to write a book about summer holidays, you can't do it in the middle of winter whilst nursing a heavy cold, slurping Lemsip and desperately trying to unblock your sinuses and remember what sunshine's like...So here I am on a sunlounger (which I practically had to kill a man to get), basking in the sunshine at my own expense, sipping sangria and swotting the flies from my crotch.

I am rather depending on you going on a holiday in search of Sunshine and a Tan. If your idea of fun is spending a fortnight sucking raw fish in a tent halfway up the Himalayas, then I suggest you put this book down now and move on to the 'Books For Nutters' section where you belong!

Normally we all start looking forward to our annual quest for the sun the minute we get back from the last one and look at all the washing there is to do. We read reports by professional travel writers who tell us about the country's sultry ambience, its traditional open-air cooking methods, and how the people stood together in times of civil war. As I'm not a travel writer, you won't be getting any of that in here. This book is about *holidays* rather than *travel*, and is seen through the (slightly neurotic) eyes of a (practically) normal punter, rather than through the rose-tinted sunglasses of one who has never had to pay.

As well as being packed with observations about every stage of your holiday, I've also tried to include things to look out for that will help you pass the time, and to see if the same types of people are in every resort or whether they just follow me everywhere.

There are tips on what to wear and how to pack it, how to spot the Holiday Bore and the Family From Hell; ideal etiquette for around the pool, and how to handle your waiters and get a free meal and a few perks. The only thing I've missed out is a good puzzle section, but you'll probably find you have enough to concentrate on with trying to suck in your stomach after eating enough paella for a family of four and endeavouring to avoid ever having to sit up in your bikini.

Right! All that's left is for me to wish you a good read and a great holiday. I would like to think that all my hard work means that you don't need to take anything else with you…but I would recommend a change of underwear…

CHAPTER ONE

Boy, Do You Need A Break!

The rain thunders down, the wind howls through the gaps in your teeth, and you find yourself yet again huddled over a two-bar electric fire in a floor-length jumper, drinking your tenth cup of coffee and eating your umpteenth slab of chocolate sponge in a vain attempt to keep warm. You're at your lowest ebb: you hate your job, you feel like sh*t, you daren't go in the bathroom in case you get frostbite, and you can't imagine life getting any worse than this. THEN you catch a glimpse of yourself in a mirror, and that tired old baggy-eyed reflection with a white-with-a-hint-of-blue glare is telling you in no uncertain terms that *YOU NEED A HOLIDAY!*

If you have any sense and money, you go off there and then; but most of us seem content to torture ourselves by scraping through the winter and waiting until the weather starts getting better here before we decide to go away. We move a bit closer to that fire and just wait for the months to drag by.

Looking through holiday brochures is one way to help you get through the winter, because if you can't afford a holiday, you can always use them to start a good fire. On your first trip to the travel agent, you're filled with hope. Your dream holiday is a huge villa with maid service and your own pool, on a quiet island in the Caribbean...but by the time you've looked through a couple of brochures you realise that all your budget will allow is a shoebox with cockroaches and your own blanket...in Beirut. Unless, of course, you go to Spain. *Again.*

11

Another thing you'll realise, and fast, is just how little you know your partner, especially if your idea of a holiday is a fortnight of sunbathing and being a Pool-Potato, and his turns out to be fly fishing in the Outer Hebrides or following Arsenal to Belgium. THEN you're in trouble. Or on separate holidays.

If you reject the mundane package destinations and have a yearning for exotic locations, prepare yourself for equally exotic injections, long flights and having to swot up on local cultural peculiarities in case there's a risk you might get arrested if your dancing is thought to be dirty, or if your elbows are an insult to Mohammed.

It also pays to be well up on world politics before you go, so there's no danger of war breaking out whilst you're there. You may scoff, but I'm the one who had a great holiday in Yugoslavia and went about recommending it as *the* place to go…What if some poor sod followed my advice at the worst possible time and his introduction to the 'friendly, accommodating' locals was with a rifle up his nose, dodging sniper fire and trying to hitch a lift in a UN truck…?

More problems pop up when you're deciding on the *type* of holiday you want. Do you want to go self-catering, or do you want a break from the kitchen? (Stupid question.) Do you want a package holiday, or are you more the Rucksack-On-My-Back type, who sneers at advance bookings and prefers to rough it under a flimsy nylon tent with only a sleeping bag for comfort?

Then you have to decide *how* you'll get there...by air, by sea, by car, by coach? You can even get there by tunnel, that is, if it's finished and working by the time this book comes out. As an awful lot of us spend far too much of our working lives sitting on Underground trains, we prefer to see a bit of scenery on our holidays. You could hire a bus à la Cliff Richard, or travel in a Daumobile – if you like the idea of spending two weeks shut in a confined space with no one to talk to but your family or partner. You might just as well draw up the divorce papers before you go.

A typically British trait is to always go to the same place every year, without fail, all of your life. Favourite places used to be Blackpool, Yarmouth or Butlins. Nowadays it's Majorca, Greece, or the Costa del Sol. You can always tell which people go to the same place every year, because the waiters know their first names and the sunloungers are moulded to the shape of their backs...

If you can live with the fact that all your friends think you're the dullest people on earth and you're content to go to the same place for the rest of your lives, fine; but if you do fancy a change and are still a bit of a coward, then try to go somewhere recommended by friends, or arrange holidays where you can spend one week somewhere new and the other in your favourite place. That way you know you'll get at least one good week.

ARGUMENTS FOR ALWAYS GOING TO THE SAME PLACE

- You always know what you're getting.
- You know all the best places to go.
- You know how much money to take.
- You always have a good time there.
- You're too scared to go anywhere else.

ARGUMENTS AGAINST

- There's no sense of adventure.
- You never get to see other parts of the world.
- You may regret being so cautious later in life.
- You always have to listen to people saying 'You're never going there *again*!'
- Everyone thinks you're Boring Old Gits.

Once you've survived the traumas of choosing your holiday, there can still be more to come, like hidden surcharges that you'll have to pay if you're not taking your entire family and half your neighbourhood with you. And then there are the small travel agents, who seem like a godsend with their more interesting choice of destinations, last-minute special offers and a service that has a more personal touch, but they are much more likely to be the ones who go bust and run off with your money. (So it's handy to try and find out where the boss lives first.) Get the magnifying glass out and check for any small print that says you're not guaranteed to have the exact type of accommodation you've paid for, or else you may find you're spending your holiday in a Portakabin in the middle of nowhere. If you manage to avoid any of these setbacks, you're still not safe, because your flight can be changed at a moment's notice, which means your leisurely lunchtime flight is now in the middle of the night and you'll arrive

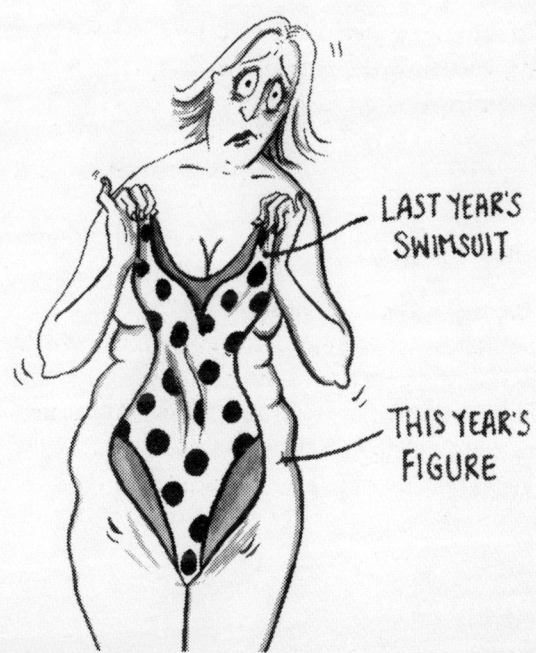

LAST YEAR'S
SWIMSUIT

THIS YEAR'S
FIGURE

feeling half dead and waste your first day wandering round in a daze.

If that isn't enough to send you straight into a nervous breakdown, you notice that the television, magazines and newspapers are suddenly full of items on what to take with you, what to wear and how to wear it…and the pressure is on to be perfectly co-ordinated. So you open your wardrobe and blow the dust off your summer clothes, only to find, as usual, a collection of garments that would look great if only you were another size or another person. Nothing matches, nothing suits you, and hardly anything fits. You have visions of yet another holiday where you take six suitcases of clothes and spend the entire time in one enormous t-shirt and a very long skirt because you hate the way you look. So what can you do?…

PERFECT HOLIDAY OUTFITS

Adapt these suggestions to suit your taste and your budget, especially if you can't afford to rush out and buy a whole new set of clothes.

TIP

Get out all your summer clothes and lie them on the bed, or on the floor, and try to make as many outfits as possible using the least amount of clothes.

The easiest holiday wardrobe is to mix two basic colours, both plain and in patterns, e.g. black and white; black and natural; navy and white; brown and cream…etc; and add a couple of bright, spangly outfits for variety.

BASIC ITEMS

- Bikini (of course).
- Hat (to protect your head when walking about and sunbathing).
- Swimsuits (as many as you like, as they don't take up much room and can double as Bodies under skirts and leggings).
- A long skirt that buttons up at the front (hides your legs in the first blotchy days, and can be gradually unbuttoned as you get browner. Or not, if you don't like your legs).
- Wide floaty trousers (are very cool, cover up your legs and are very glamorous in the evenings).
- Shorts (cycling, cut off jeans, whatever your taste is).
- Sarong (to cover up by the pool and for evenings).
- T-shirts (for covering up when walking about, and a big one for covering up sunburn by the pool).
- Big loose shirts (worn over swimsuit and leggings, skirts, etc; a good excuse for colourful patterns).
- Jacket (worn when you travel, and handy for any sudden chilly nights).
- A couple of glam tops (silk, see-through, sparkly, etc).
- A dress (long and floaty or short and sassy).
- Espadrilles, evening sandals and the obligatory flip-flops...
- Accessories: bracelets, earrings, necklaces...to get dressed up with.
  (If you are really broke, and can't even afford to buy one necklace or one new top, borrow something from a friend, so you at least *feel* like you've got something new.)

Once you've sorted out which clothes to take, try and imagine when you'll wear them: for morning walks, sunbathing by the pool, and for evening posing. Try and wear things more than once, but with something different each time so everyone will think you brought all your wardrobe with you.

PACKING TIPS

Watch out for fabrics that crease easily, such as silk, linen and pure cotton. You could have spent a fortune on a linen suit, but it will look like a dishcloth after an hour's wear or a bit of bad packing. Try mixtures of man-made fibres with natural ones, as they reduce creasing, and some polyester tops can look just as glamorous as silk, but are practically impossible to crease. Take a travel iron with you if you insist on taking creasable clothes, or enquire whether the maid service also offers ironing, which will certainly save you the bother.

The age old favourite way of getting the creases out of clothes is to hang them up in the bathroom whilst you bath and let the steam do the work. DON'T do what a friend of mine did, and hang them on an unstable hook only to have them drop in the bath and all the colours run together, ruining her best clothes on the first day!

The best tip I can give you is to remember that the ideal holiday clothes are loose and light and cool. The last thing you want are tight, ill-fitting clothes that not only make you twice as hot, but will also cling to any bits of spare flab and make you feel completely miserable. A holiday can be one of the few excuses you get to be a bit of a glamour queen in the evenings, so *go for it*!

I know all this sorting out seems like an awful lot of bother, but it shouldn't take too long, especially if you get a friend in to help you over a cup of coffee or a stiff gin, depending on how depressed you get looking at your clothes.

Right. That's your clothes sorted, now which bags will you take them in? Will it be those embarrassing flowered ones you had for your eighteenth birthday; something a lot more trendy but in danger of collapsing before you get to the airport; or one of those huge, sturdy, sensible cases that weighs a ton before you get your clothes in, and needs a fork lift truck to get it off the bed?

When there's just yourself to pack for, the best bags are those nylon tube ones. You can roll up all your clothes and cram absolutely loads in, which also makes the bag a lot sturdier. The only risk is that someone's Samsonite will get hurled on top of it and, although the bag will stand the strain, all your hair gel will explode over your clothes. Then you'll wish you hadn't scoffed at those items on Daytime TV that told you to put your toiletries in a plastic bag...

When you're travelling with children you'll need as much room as you can get. Even a trip to Granny's needs an articulated lorry to carry all the bags you have to take, so those enormous everything-but-the-kitchen-sink bags are best. (You can always go on a weight lifting course to help you lug the thing about.)

When you're travelling with one of those men who is incapable of buying his own clothes, who hasn't got a clue where underpants come from and who expects his case to get miraculously packed without him even touching a sock...just screw it all up in a carrier bag and see how long it takes before he notices.

Packing isn't a straightforward task. It takes careful planning, list-making and a few practice runs so you know there'll be enough room for everything. In an ideal world, that is. Usually you find that the bag is sitting on the floor already bursting at the seams, and all you've put in is your suncream, or you've packed a few days in advance and slapped yourself on the back for being so efficient...but when the taxi arrives to take you to the station, you can't lift it off the floor. So at least try it once before you go...to save you from any headaches or hernias.

Losing your luggage is one of your biggest worries when travelling abroad. You're loath to take all your favourite things in case they disappear, and scared to leave them at home in case you're burgled. The best thing you can do is to mix your clothes in with your partners, so you at least have something to wear if one bag gets lost. We are assured these days that bags seldom go astray, but if they do, a computer will always find them. You can't have them, of course, but at least you know where they are.

As if you haven't got enough to worry about, people have now started observing that the way you pack reveals an awful lot about your personality. This makes you a nervous wreck in case someone wants to search your bags at the airport and discovers what a SLOB you are, or else you get deeply disappointed that no one did and you can't show off. Either way, as you walk round the airport you're terrified in case the way you've tied your labels says TERRORIST, and you'll be whipped off for a quick strip search...

ESSENTIAL ITEMS TO PACK

- Some form of first aid kit, adapted to whether you'll be facing wild animals on a safari or tackling a couple of mosquitos in your bedroom.
- A phrase book, so you can try and order meals in the language. It's also advisable to learn a couple of helpful phrases ('I'm married'...'I've already *had* my appendix out')...just in case.
- Something to stop you from going to the toilet, if your stomach reacts to the change in diet or a poison paella. (You can spot the people with this trouble – they can't sit still for long, and they sit very, very close to the toilets.)
- Something to help you to *go* to the toilet. (These are very easy to spot too – they're the ones walking round after four or five days clutching their stomachs and racing to the shops to buy up all the All-Bran.)

All that's left now is to sort out your hand luggage. I can't really understand why airlines bother to say we're only allowed one piece of hand luggage, because everyone else always seems to have at least five, all bigger than the one I checked in with, and usually crammed into the compartment above my head.

Your passport, purse and foreign money are better off in a bum-bag in case your bag gets pinched at the airport. (I don't know what happens if your bum gets pinched…) This way you won't be forever sorting through your hand luggage every time you want to buy something.

WHAT TO HAVE IN YOUR HAND LUGGAGE

- Camera, film, batteries.
- Pills in case of headache or sickness.
- A soft drink, like Mineral water, in case the service is slow and you're desperate for a drink.
- Personal stereo in case the film's crap or you're anywhere near the Family From Hell.
- A spare swimsuit, a pair of leggings and a change of underwear in case all your luggage goes missing or you crash somewhere without a shop.
- A book. This one preferably, or any one written by me.

BOOKS TO AVOID

- Any heavy, large books like *War and Peace*, as you won't get anything else in.
- *The Ozone and You … The A–Z of Skin Cancer … What's That Floating in the Sea?*
- *Eight Miles Up and Only One Engine…*

Well, I think that's it. You should be packed, organised and ready to go. You'll have a list of everything you're taking, you'll be wearing something comfortable to travel in, and you'll actually be able to lift your bag off the floor. You can't carry it anywhere, but that's what taxis and trolleys are for.

Now you're ready for the *airport*!

CHAPTER TWO

I wish it wasn't called a terminal...

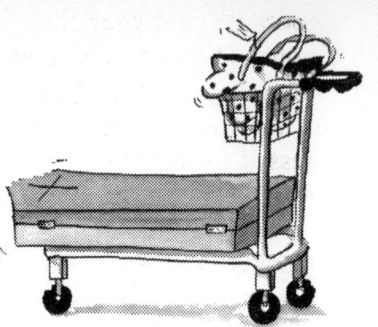

As soon as you arrive at the airport your nerves automatically start to twitch. On your way in you saw a plane land and you're convinced that its wheels scraped the top of the trees. You try to calm yourself with the thought that hundreds of planes come and go from this airport every day, and you're much more likely to die in a motorway pile-up or a train crash than you are on a plane. (Cheering thoughts for your journey home.)

You decided in the end to take the trendy lightweight bag because it looks better and it goes with what you're wearing. It's lasting very well so far. You've only had to call in at WH Smith on the way to get some string to hold it together and some Superglue to stick the handle back on, but apart from that, it's been fine...

On your way up the escalator you begin to panic. You're convinced that you've left the oven on, the back door wide open, and that the neighbours will leave your cat to starve whilst squandering your money on drink and parties rather than on catfood. As well as that, you're beginning to regret what you've put on to travel in. Your shoes are too high, your jacket's a bit too tight and your skirt is starting to ride up towards your neck, and as both your hands are full there's nothing you can do about it.

As you approach the check-in area, you are possessed with something which affects even the most mild-mannered, placid and patient people...you're transformed into a snarling, shoving, spitting, Must-Get-To-The-Desk-First MONSTER with the belief that everyone else is Out To Get Your Seat. You start eyeing up the people around you, assessing how many children they have, how big a group they're in and how many less seats there will be by the time you get there if you don't get a move on. You start walking faster, snapping at your partner, falling over in your shoes and tearing up the ankles of anyone who gets in your way. Once you've drawn blood there'll be no stopping you.

You have arrived three hours early and already the queue is half a mile long. You pinpoint one group in particular that you really have to get past. There's at least ten of them, all with two children apiece, and they've spotted you trying to overtake them. The race is on. They send one of the kids ahead to grab a place in the queue, you decide to really put your foot down...and your trolley decides to go in the opposite direction. By the time you stop you're halfway to customs, and not only has that family got in front of you, but *four* others too. No wonder most people arrive at the end of the queue ready to murder everyone in sight...

CHECKING IN

For people with children this can turn into a nightmare. Especially if you've already had a long journey and the kids have decided that if they can't sit down or eat chips, then they are going to make your life a MISERY. Without children it's just a drag, but it can become a nightmare if you're stuck behind some who have decided to play up in a big way...or if you're anywhere near a Family From Hell...You must have encountered at least one of these on your holidays, unless you have been extremely lucky or walking round with your eyes shut.

The Family From Hell normally comes in two types:

LARGE, LOUD AND LAWLESS

- They're a sprawling mass of children, luggage and tattoos. They always travel in large groups of at least three families and they're the ones who push to the front of the queue, turn round and say, '*WHATCH-ERGONNADOABOUTIT?*' They smoke in no-smoking areas, the children are always screaming and there's no attempt at discipline apart from the occasional half-hearted, 'Don't set fire to the lady's dress, Darren...' and wherever they are, they spread out like a bad rash, taking at least three seats apiece.

Almost as bad are the

LAID BACK LIBERALS

- These say, when their children are running round, spilling their drinks over everyone, that they are Releasing Their Inner Frustrations. When they're drawing on the airport walls they're simply Expressing Themselves. When they're charging up and down the aisle of the plane and fiddling with the exit doors they're Naturally Curious, and when they're screaming the same song over and over and over again, they think it's just Too Sweet For Words. They don't believe in suppressing a child's natural behaviour and would never dream of giving them a darned good hiding. Everyone else does, though…

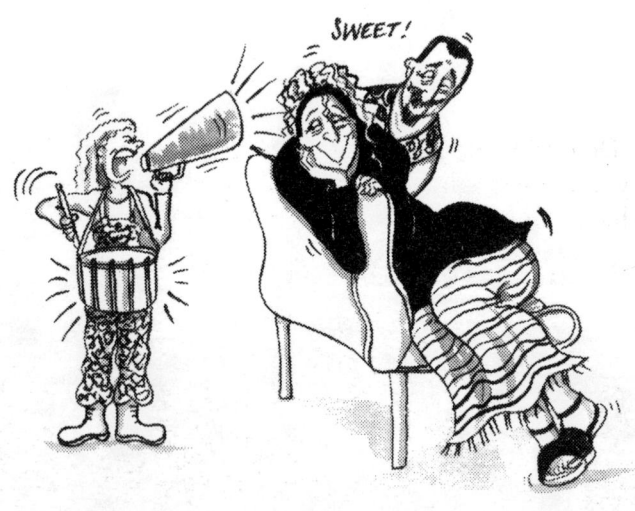

Both families are a complete pain in the neck, and if you are unlucky enough to get both types on one holiday, I should rush to the airport pharmacy and stock up on the sedatives…

Back to checking in…When you're standing in the queue with nothing better to do, have a good look at your fellow passengers. Not only will they be on the same flight as you, but they could be in the seat next to you. They could even be going to the same resort and end up in the apartment next to you. Fingers crossed it's not the group of Lads with three ghetto blasters…each.

Depending on how long you're there, you could also try and guess which women will be going topless and which will be clinging to their tops for dear life...

...which men will be walking round eyeballing your nipples (they're probably doing it already)...and which men will have bigger breasts than their wives...

My biggest fear when flying (apart from a slow death in the deep blue sea), is ending up in the smoking seats. I can't believe that people are still allowed to smoke on a plane. It's bad enough being in a confined space miles up in the air with no hope of escape, without being surrounded by people knocking back the duty-frees and waving lit fags about…So I'm one of those people who would camp out overnight if it guaranteed me a seat at the front. Once I'm sure that I've got a seat as far away from the fags as possible without actually being in the cockpit, I can start to relax a bit and enjoy the delights of the airport.

The mere fact that airport shops are filled with things to buy in case you've forgotten anything, automatically makes you think that you have, so you could easily spend most of your money there in a blind panic. A cheaper alternative is to spend a smaller amount on some food, as you've nearly always had to miss one meal to get there; so you can pass some time sitting down filling your face before you get to sit on a plane and fill it some more.

The general impression you get from airport restaurants is that, as you only eat there once a year, what difference does it make if the food is crap and the coffee so strong that it'll keep you awake for a week? You're hardly going back there the next day to complain are you? Your best bet is to stick to food that doesn't look like it's been sitting under a heat lamp since the last time you were there, and steer clear of fry-ups with baked beans if you're on the same flight as me. You may want to have a hearty meal because you think it might be your last, or that it doesn't matter what you eat because the way you feel it'll all end up down the toilet anyway.

A popular way to compensate for the taste of the food is to disappear into the bar and drown yourself in drink. Some people, me included, need to be slightly squiffy in order to get through the flight, but if you drink too much alcohol they can refuse to let you on the plane as you become a security risk (especially if you like to get up and dance) or else you become this year's annoying berk who keeps spoiling everyone's view of the film because you have to keep getting up to go to the toilet.

AIRPORT CHECKLIST

Is there:

- A couple who have started snogging already?
- A gang of lively old pensioners in light blue slacks and lilac velour tracksuits?
- Someone on their own who looks like a terrorist?
- Someone on their own who looks like she's doing a Shirley Valentine?
- A couple of girls who really think that Pedro and Diego are still waiting for them?
- A group of men who are drunk at nine in the morning?
- A couple who aren't talking to each other?

The usual step after eating is to have a look round the shops, unless your flight is delayed and then you'll be straight back in the bar...

If you have been fairly well organised, you won't need to buy any books or tapes or socks, but you will anyway, because they're there. Once you get tired of looking at the same old shops, you'll probably be in need of a change of scenery, so move through to the departure lounge and look at a few different ones. It does mean, however, that you're heading for the most embarrassing part of your trip...where your passport photo gets its annual airing and you get to see your pantie-liners shining out from the x-ray machine. It can also be the time when your bag gets hauled up and searched because the headphones from your personal stereo have got wrapped round the pot of Vaseline you put in at the last minute (in case your lips got dry on the plane, honest)...and it looks like a primitive bomb. So not only do you have to stand sheepishly in front of them trying to look as unlike a terrorist as possible, you also have to endure their waving the tub about for all the airport to see, wishing fervently that you'd put the lipsalve in instead.

Now passport control looms. You look at the photo that's staring back at you. It's got totally different hair, embarrassing make-up and looks like Olive Oyl on acid. Just as you think they're going to start passing it round for a laugh, some woman's Wonderbra sets off the metal detector, their attention is diverted, and you slip through without so much as a smirk.

As this will be your last chance to spend money in Blighty, they don't miss a trick in trying to wrench all your holiday cash from you before you're even on the plane. I think airports do a deal with air traffic control, to delay the flights as much as possible, so you have nothing else to do but spend your money and count all the hours of tanning time you're losing. If the selection

of video games doesn't tempt your money out of your trousers, they'll try their best in the duty-free shop. I'm never that impressed with duty-frees, because I want them to be more free than duty; and as I don't smoke and don't fancy carting huge heavy bottles of booze on the plane, I just tend to wander aimlessly about dodging any perfume salesgirl whose mission in life is to make me spend the first few hours of my holiday smelling like an old tart.

After another walk round the shops and another cup of coffee you'll probably find, delays permitting, that you only have enough time for a quick fight over the seats with the Family From Hell and a few more trips to the loo before they announce your departure gate and you go through to the final stage before getting on the plane.

If you're not already racked with nerves, this place will soon set you off a treat because all you get to look

THINGS YOU DON'T WANT TO SEE AT THE AIRPORT...(1)

at are planes, planes and more planes. You see planes take off and land, you see the luggage being thrown – sorry – loaded on board the plane, you can even see the pilots walking round the plane on the tarmac to prove they're sober. You could always try turning your back, shutting your eyes and pretending you're going on a train...but your stomach has already started churning because the toilets are just that bit too far away and you *know* that the minute you decide to go, you'll be called to board the plane and you'll be the one who holds everyone up.

Time ticks by, and the atmosphere is getting heavier and heavier. It could be with the presence of so much nervous energy, but it's much more likely to be because all the smokers are puffing away like mad, as it'll be at least twenty minutes before they can light up again.

THINGS YOU DON'T WANT TO SEE AT THE AIRPORT...(2)

A member of the airport staff makes an announcement, and is holding up a bag. Is it yours? Are they criticising it because they think it clashes with the company colour scheme...or are they saying it'll never last the journey, the handle's come off again, and you really should have brought that nice flowery case your mother gave you? No, it's not yours, thankfully, it's a big canvas rucksack that hasn't got any labels on, so it's a security risk, and they're waiting for the owner to come forward. Everyone looks around to see what a true twit looks like, and you wait...and wait...and wait. Eventually a hippy student emerges from a corner and slouches casually over to claim the bag, completely oblivious to all the eyes burning into his back. Now, you know *you'd* rather leave the bag behind than admit to being such a berk, but he just shrugs his shoulders and goes back to

his seat, whilst the rest of you make a mental note to clip him on the back of the head whenever you walk past his seat on the plane.

Now you start to board. Disabled people and babies first. The babies alone should take at least an hour...and then you go by seat numbers, until your number is up (so to speak) and your wobbly legs carry you through the doors. Thankfully the walk to the plane is in one of those covered walkways, which is a bit like going into the House Of Fun at the seaside. Only this cost a lot more and you won't be able to leave if you feel sick. At least you can't look at the plane and start imagining that you can see huge gaping cracks and that the wings are held on with Sellotape. You're getting nearer and nearer. The plane is humming with the sound of children who have just about had enough and who are beginning to think they're never going to get this holiday they've been blackmailed with for the past few months. In front of you there's a pensioner who's started his air crash stories, one man looks like his legs are collapsing from fear (or is it lager?)...and you want another wee. There's no going back now, the stewardess has made eye contact with you and has started to smile...

CHAPTER THREE

Why isn't that stewardess a bodybuilder?

FAR TOO WEEDY!

You're on the plane. The stewardess has smiled her ten thousandth smile and she's only been there five minutes. You try to move down the aisle to your seat, dodging flying hand luggage and rampaging children. If the position of your seat is an important factor for your surviving the flight without having a nervous breakdown or committing murder, then you should have sorted it out at the check-in desk: it's too late now. If you want an aisle seat with a perfect view of the film which is also near a toilet and some exit doors, then say so. You don't stand much chance of getting it, but at least you tried.

If you're disabled or infirm, you always get a seat right at the front, which is a bit unfortunate as all you get to look at is a lousy view of the film and a great view of the toilets.

GOOD SEATS

- Aisle seats for those with long legs or who feel squashed next to a window.
- Window seats for those who want to look at the view, which is rather spectacular if you don't mind being reminded of how high up you are.
- By the middle exit doors. Not only darned handy in case of emergencies, but there's also lots of room to stretch your legs.

I USUALLY get 2 seats to myself

BAD SEATS

- Any ones if you're over three foot two.
- In the middle of a row, between two large strangers, or next to someone who can't eat their complimentary meal with their mouth shut.
- Behind, in front of, or anywhere near the Family From Hell.
- In a seat that doesn't go back, but the ones in front do.
- Near an engine, in with the smokers, miles from an exit or directly under a video screen.
- Next to the man with the engine failure stories.

I like to keep my hand luggage with me...

It's nice when the boys find a friend....

I'm 3 rows away from the smoking seats, and that's near enough for ME!

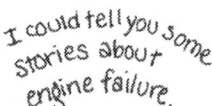
I could tell you some stories about engine failure...

It's Baby's first flight. Isn't he DUCKY? WAAAH!

MY LIFE STORY VOL.1

No matter where your seat is, within a few minutes you'll find it's too narrow, incredibly prickly, and your neck will be stiff from the headrest. You could always try one of those inflatable pillows, which are supposed to make you much more comfortable. Unfortunately they also give you instant fat cheeks and an enormous double chin, so you have to choose between having a bit of a stiff neck, or a face like a baboon…

Now your pilot should be making himself known to you. As an unashamed uniform fetishist, I like to build up an image of what he'll look like…a tall dashing man with shiny buttons and a deep tan, his strong manly arms skilfully handling his joystick and being perfectly in control. His name is very important to neurotic fliers, because it has to exude confidence. Names like Captain Scott, Captain Denham, and Captain Grant make you instantly at ease. Last year our pilot said, 'Hello, my name is Captain Mick Smith.' It just wasn't the same…

As the plane moves along the runway to get into take-off position, the stewardesses will begin the safety demonstration. Forget the old days of robotic arm movements and blank faces, these days you also get a video to watch, which gives you an idea of what might actually happen in an emergency, instead of leaving you to decipher the drawings on the safety sheet. (Except for the fact that everyone in the video has perfect composure and acts like a responsible adult, whereas we all know in reality there'd be one great big fist-fight to get to the exit doors.)

They may have updated their equipment, but they still cling to their traditional routine, like the Crash Position, which doesn't seem at all wise to me, to have

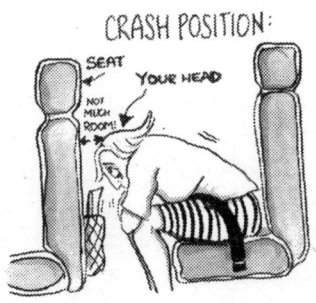

your head rammed up against the back of the seat in front. And so what if there are lights to guide you down the aisle? They're going to do you a LOT of good as you're hurling towards the sea at xxx miles an hour. The most unnerving safety aspect has to be the flimsy protection of your seat belt, which only straps across your hips, and makes you realise that you get more protection at Alton Towers than you do on a plane.

And what about stewardesses? When I'm on a plane, I want to see women with Madonna-like muscles, who are capable of hauling me from the sea in a gale force storm, not these bony-armed waifs who look like they'd collapse if their mascara ran. So what if they can speak pigeon French? If they can't get me into a lifeboat, they're in the wrong job!

Let's face it, though, if you crash, you crash, and there's not a lot you can do about it. Except make sure you climb over everyone else to get to the exit doors first...

Once the safety demonstration's over, the stewardesses sit down, and you're ready for take-off, which I quite enjoy. It's just the hours in the air that I can't handle. Apparently, the take-off and landings are the most interesting part of the flight for the pilots, which I find very reassuring. Just as long as they don't get too bored and fall asleep.

As you climb into the air, ears a-popping, there are a couple of noises you might hear which could cause you a lot of alarm if you don't know what they are. (I read about them in the in-flight magazine in an article called 'Things That Go Bump In The Flight.') Firstly, the big loud clunk is the sound of the wheels going in and not a wing dropping off...and then the engine will suddenly go very quiet, as if it has stopped altogether. This is just an anti-noise device for the houses below, and doesn't mean you'll soon be dropping into their gardens...

In a couple of minutes the stewardesses will be up and about with the first round of drinks. My advice is to BUY SOME. It's amazing how quickly the flight passes and how stress-free it can be after a couple of gins and a complimentary Bucks Fizz.

IN-FLIGHT ENTERTAINMENT

As you're knocking back your drink, you can settle down to enjoy the film. If you can see the screen, that is. Some planes have several small screens, which I prefer, especially after last year when there was just the one large screen for everyone, and wouldn't you know it, the mum from the Family From Hell was smack bang in the middle, complete with mile-high hair filled with huge wide bows and which her children (all standing up, of course) were brushing all the way through. If it's not your view that gets disturbed, you may find your attention is distracted by someone's baby in the

YOUR VIEW OF THE FILM....

seat in front, who wants you to play 'Peep-bo' with it. For hours. Not only that, but you are expected to smile sweetly as it decides to wipe its Mars Bar in your hair and spit its drink in your face. Otherwise you're a miserable old witch in the eyes of the entire family, who have turned round to look at you. Not just because you have spurned the attentions of their angel child, but it now means they have to find another way to keep it amused.

FILMS YOU DON'T WANT TO SEE

- *Airport 1977*
- *The Buddy Holly Story*
- *The Glenn Miller Story*
- *The Dambusters*

If your flight doesn't offer you a film, or if the video isn't working, you'll have to pass the time in another way. You could try and sleep, which is always a bit tricky with one knee in your chest and someone else's elbow up your nose. You could listen to all your holiday tapes or read most of your books, which will leave you with nothing to do when you're sunbathing. You could listen to the in-flight radio which plays a variety of music, from pop, to classical and even some hits from the Middle Ages! They may provide a comedy channel, which is a great way to pass the time, unless the clips are linked by someone who isn't in the least bit funny. You could always read the in-flight magazine. Again. Or you could watch the stewardesses running up and down the aisles to attend to the Family From Hell and keep its children from eating the seats...or you could listen to the pilots, who are now really bored and have started telling you weather reports, cricket results, and which storylines you'll miss in *EastEnders*. You could even play 'What's That Odour?'...But most fun of all has to be counting the numbers of grey hairs on the head of the man who has fallen asleep on your chest, and trying to guess how long it'll take before he dribbles in your lap.

The dishing out, eating and collecting up of the meal should take up a good chunk of the flight. If you're near the front of the plane you get to choose which course you eat, but by the time they get to row twenty, all the pasta has gone and everyone else is left with something called Chicken Surprise, but which looks more like Shocked Spam. If you have ordered a vegetarian meal, I shouldn't be too surprised if it isn't there. Unless you get it written in blood when you book it, you'll probably find yourself having a conversation with the stewardess where she says, 'Did you order a vegetarian meal?' and you say, 'Yes', and she checks her list and says, 'Are you sure?' and you say, 'No, I'm a complete idiot'…and then she'll run away, returning with a meal which, she says, 'Hasn't got *much* meat in it…'

The most bizarre thing about airline meals is that they never seem to adapt to the time of day. One year our flight was so late it meant we were eating after midnight, so everyone was wondering what we'd get to eat. Cocoa and biscuits? Cornflakes? Nope. We got shepherd's pie followed by apple crumble and custard. We all hoped even more than usual that we wouldn't have any emergencies, because we'd never have got out of our seats.

Of course, if you've ever seen one of those disaster movies you'll be tempted to skip the meal altogether in case you get the food poisoning...but I think you're better off getting it, because otherwise if you're the only healthy person on the plane, it'll be you who they ask to land the damned thing!

In my experience, as soon as the meal is in front of me, the TURBULENCE will start. Maybe it's just nature's way of protecting my stomach, because it never fails to put me right off. All I can manage is the bottle of wine and the dessert. It takes an awful lot to put me off a dessert, especially a free one. In fact, if it came to a choice between having to adopt the crash position or plummeting towards the sea eating my dessert, I know which I'd choose. If I'm going to go, it'll be with the taste of the nondescript chocolate-type sponge thing in my mouth...Sometimes the turbulence is no worse than travelling on Network Southeast or on an old bus when the roads are up. Other times it's enough to make couples hold hands when they haven't done it for years, for people to pray when they've never done it before, and even to make the kids quiet for the first time since they left the house. This is the time when stewardesses become really useful. If *they* start to look worried, you're in trouble; but most of the time they just carry on as normal and the only thing you have to worry about is whether they'll spill your coffee in your lap. Unless, of course, they're pretending...

When the meal is over, there will be just enough time for you to wipe the damp mascara from your cheeks, as the film is nearly always a soppy one (the stewardesses need their entertainment too, like making bets to see who'll blub first), for the man next to you to have a quick nap on your lap, and for the child in the seat behind to have a really good kick at the back of yours.

There's not much to occupy your sight apart from watching all the people hopping about in the aisles who are desperate for the loo but are stuck behind the last duty-free trolleys...or you could compile your *On The Plane* checklist...

ON THE PLANE CHECKLIST

Is there:

- An old man who keeps going to the loo?
- Someone nearby who hasn't washed their espadrilles since last year?
- Someone's child making one last attempt to give you a migraine?
- A great, big, butch bloke sitting in the stewardesses' seat with his head in his hands because flying makes him feel really, really sick?

At last you're approaching your destination. There will be rejoicing in the cockpit, as the pilots now have something to do as the plane begins its descent. They have buttons to press, switches to flick and a landing to make.

You sit back in your seat without a thing to worry about. Except why do you always pick places where the runway is surrounded by sea? As you come further and further down, all you can see is water, and lots of it. You think the pilot is going to miss. You desperately try to remember where they said the life jacket was...and then suddenly there's land. Gorgeous, wonderful, FIRM land!

Planes land here every 30 seconds ...We've been sitting here for a minute and a half...it's a miracle we're still ALIVE!

You're so happy you could almost forgive the child behind for your bruised coccyx...but not quite. Everyone forgets the promises they made during the turbulence, and all the things they wanted to do to the Family From Hell. They even forget to clip the Hippy one more time on the back of the head because they're on foreign soil, the sun is out, and when there isn't a war it can only mean one thing...*you're on your HOLIDAYS!*

Unfortunately, your first holiday experience will be being jammed up against someone's armpit in the sardine can they call a coach, on the ride to the airport terminal...but even *that* you can take...

CHAPTER FOUR

I am a great white whale...

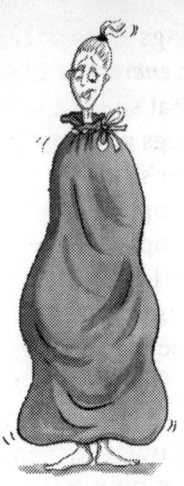

On your way across the tarmac in the bus, you will notice that you are being stared at from the windows of the departure lounge. You may think it's out of pure envy because these people are going home and you have only just arrived...but you'd be wrong. They're looking at you to see how PALE you are. The paler you are, the worse the weather is back home, and the better they can flaunt their tans...

There are no worries at this airport about having your passport photo held up to ridicule or being refused entry to the country because it doesn't look anything like you; because these boys hardly look at your passport at all. In fact, security can be so slack that you begin to think the x-ray machines and metal detectors are cardboard cutouts and only there for effect. International drug smugglers would only have to put on a pair of touristy shorts and they'd sail through. Still, you get through quickly, and that's all you're bothered about when you're starting your holidays.

As you stand at the conveyor belt waiting for the

bags to appear, feeling a bit like a guest on the *Generation Game* (only without the prizes) you have that sinking feeling that this will be the year when your bags go missing and you'll be forced to wear your partner's clothes all holiday. You begin to wish you'd gone shopping with him instead of letting him loose in a shop on his own, and just as you're trying to work out 101 ways to wear one 'Viz' T-shirt and a pair of ghastly tropical shorts, the conveyor belt starts to move, and the bags begin to appear.

The first thing you notice is how filthy the bags are, as if they had been dragged behind the plane the whole way. Then you notice that the Family From Hell has not only forced its way to the best spot, but that their bags are the first out. Bag after bag passes by, including one that has been going round for ages and no one has claimed, which means that the same lazy family go wherever I do every year, or else each conveyor belt has one lonely bag that keeps going round and round until its owners eventually return there.

As they go round, you look at the things people do to their bags to make them instantly recognisable. Some have belts with their names printed on, others favour bright scarves, or write their names using bits of sticky tape. Well, you tied a scarf *and* wrote your name with the brightest tape possible and *still* you can't see it. To make matters worse, your partner's has arrived, and they went on together, didn't they? So what's keeping it? You begin to imagine your bag sitting alone on the Tarmac at Gatwick, or halfway to Bangkok; or perhaps the stewardesses are at this moment sewing up the seams in your swimsuits to make you feel twice as fat just because you laughed at their blue eye-shadow...You decide to grab the next bag that looks remotely like yours and make a run for it...and then you see it coming down the chute. Just as someone's Samsonite crashes down on top of it.

You're almost ready, apart from one thing, which you've been trying to put off for ages...your first visit to a foreign loo. The trip to your resort will be at least an hour long on a coach, so there's no avoiding it. If you've never been abroad before, you'll probably be expecting a dingy, wet-floored, no-room-to-swing-a-tampon type of affair, but you usually find they're a darned sight cleaner than the ones in your local shopping centre...

At last you're ready to whizz through customs, go through to arrivals and *MEET YOUR REP*.

Anyone who has ever been on a package holiday will have an opinion on Reps. Unless they've had their life saved by one or have actually met one who could speak the language, most people would agree that they'd like to get them all in a group and *shoot them*. (If only they could find them...)

Reps are very easy to spot. At the airport they're the ones in the gaudy outfits waving their company clipboards and ticking you off their lists; on the coach they're the ones in the gaudy outfits spitting at you through the microphone at the tops of their voices...and from then on they're the ones in the gaudy outfits who talk to you as if you were a five-year-old child who is hard of hearing and brain dead.

They're very popular with old ladies, because they're the only people left in the world who smile for no good reason, except long term residents in mental homes. There's nothing wrong with smiling, of course, only

these smiles come straight from the teeth, because it's been part of their training. There's rarely any sign of real emotion going on, which is why so many people want to hit them, just to see a reaction that hasn't been covered in their training course. Also part of the training course appears to be an obsession for starting every conversation with '*Basically...*' and ending it with '*...Okay?*'

Female Reps wear dresses and skirts because they are girls, topped off with a scarf in the company colours, which are usually those that nobody with any taste would willingly put together in daylight. It amazes me why they wear a scarf at all, in hot climates...unless it's to give us something to GAG them with when they start to get on our nerves...

Male Reps tend to look like rejects from *Baywatch* whose hi-lites didn't come up to scratch. Either that, or they have that 'wacky' look reserved for children's television presenters and someone on hard drugs, topped off with haircuts that look like they stick their fingers in electric sockets, just for a laugh...The failed beach bums tend to get most of the girls, although the wacky ones may get lucky if there's someone on the rebound who has had a LOT to drink and actually thinks he's funny. The gay ones just get surrounded by grannies who can't understand why all young men aren't as pleasant and well-groomed as they are.

Back to the airport; and you can tell which one is your Rep because she's squealing the company name out at everyone who passes and nearly had your eye out with her clipboard. You get yourself a seat on the coach and wait for her to 'Rope in the rest of the gang...' Once she's on, she'll introduce herself, '*I'm Sammi*'...and start spitting into the microphone as the coach moves away.

If companies are going to insist that their Reps force their throats on us, why don't they give them a quick course in how to use a microphone? And anyway, why do they have to talk to us at all? Depending on what time you land and what your flight was like, the witterings of overly pleasant nitwits will either be tolerated, endured or downright resented. Rarely will they be the highlight of your trip. I once landed at midnight, and sat on a coach filled with a large number of very tired children and completely knackered adults, all of whom were fast asleep or were just dropping off, when 'Kirsty' bellowed out, 'WE-LL...AND I THOUGHT THE GATWICK CROWD WERE SUPPOSED TO BE *LIVELY*!' All of the babies promptly woke up and quite rightly started screaming, and all the

adults instantly got headaches. Kirsty continued for another hour, describing all the sights on 'This lovely island' that we couldn't see because it was the middle of the night, but which she had to say because it was her job...and was lucky to leave the coach alive.

A favourite part of the Reps' job is trying to get you to go on as many trips as possible, which all cost the earth and from which, I suspect, they earn nice little commissions. That's why they're so keen to get you to go to the morning 'Hello' meeting, so they can ply you with drink and get you to part with your money.

As you eventually pull into Sun Paradise (where there isn't any sun and it sure don't look like paradise...), Sammi tries to make eye contact with you and get your name down for the meeting (which always seems to be at the crack of dawn) so you'll feel morally obliged to go.

By now you'll be feeling like a nice cup of tea, which you won't get until you're home, because even if you bring your favourite teabags with you, the milk is never quite the same. Nevertheless, a cup of tea of sorts is the best thing to have as you sit on your balcony or patio and survey the area. Unless you realise that you have the one apartment that's next to the generator or above the disco, and then tea will have to wait as you shoot down to reception to get yourself moved.

Either way, once you've worked out how to get the water to work, the electricity on and have unpacked your bags, you'll be just about ready to collapse.

APARTMENT CHECKLIST

Are you:

- Near the disco, the generator...or both?
- Next to a Family From Hell, who have a *huge* amount of children, all of whom are training to be town criers?
- Next to the local family who have brought their large and rather anti-social dog?
- Next to a couple who roll in from the 'English Pub' every night at three am, have sex to the rhythm of their ghetto blaster... and make you long for the generator?

The first morning you wake up with the sun pouring through your curtains. You feel rejuvenated, you leap out of bed to greet the day and soak up a few rays. Unfortunately there's a floor-length mirror right in front of you. You thought you looked pale at home, but in bright foreign sunshine you're positively *luminous*! You look down from your balcony and everyone you see is at least tinged with brown and you are a great, fat, lily-white *whale*. You couldn't possibly face stripping off just yet, so you decide to go to the Reps' meeting instead.

In case you've never been to one, this is an opportunity to meet some fellow holidaymakers, learn a little about the country, and get another look at your Reps, in case you should ever need them. It's also a good excuse to get drunk for nothing. For the Reps, it's their chance to plug their trips and get away with telling you as little as possible. They talk about the resort (briefly), the history of the country (briefly), and which trips they have on offer (in glorious detail). Normally the type of trips they have will depend on where you go;

the Canaries offer camel rides, volcano sightseeing, and boat trips; the Costa del Sol offers bullfights, waterparks and a chance to look at a lot of timeshares. All come with (surprise, surprise) an opportunity to spend money in shops and restaurants along the way.

Most fun of all (and which I suffered for the sake of this book) is the *Night Out With Your Rep*s; where they ship you off somewhere incredibly remote (so you can't escape) with the promise of a free meal and as much wine as you can drink (providing it's not much, as it always runs out halfway)...and to top it all, the Reps will put on a show for you. This they make up themselves, all by themselves, and with no help from anyone with a sense of humour. Now, if you think I'm being unnecessarily harsh, remember that I have been there, seen the show and heard the jokes! And if you don't trust my judgement, just take a look through the Company Book (which is always in reception in case a Rep isn't available) and read the many witticisms

penned by the Reps, which they normally do in crayons and felt-tips, and which are accompanied by drawings that are so bad a two-year-old with a bad hand could beat the pants off them. Have a good, long read, and you'll get an idea of just how funny the show's going to be...

One of the most nauseating aspects of the Reps' meeting is their complete inability to stray from their memorised speech. Any sudden, impromptu questions completely throw them, and you have to wait until they've reached the end before they can answer you.

Even if you're not particularly bothered about asking questions, it's worth doing it just to watch them sweat. I think they include that tedious section on the history of the country just to put you in a daze so you don't notice that they aren't telling you anything you actually want to know, like how much meals cost in general, handy phrases for ordering food, or how to spot the Timeshare Touts before they spot you.

KNOCK KNOCK!
(Who's there?)
REP!
(Rep who?)
O COME ON, YOU MET ME ON THE COACH ON THURSDAY! YOU CAN'T HAVE FORGOTTEN ME ALREADY, HEH HEH HEH HEH

Ask how to get your cooker working or your shower fixed, and you won't see them for dust...hint that you might be interested in one of their trips and they'll be round like a shot. Which they all should be.

After a couple of drinks, however, you've forgotten

all the things you meant to ask this year, and are feeling so contented and squiffy that you even begin to think their uniforms are attractive.

After the meeting you'll probably want to explore the area. (If you can stand up.) As you walk around feeling like Mr Blobby's pale relation, there are two things you will want to see, and fast. Firstly, an awful lot of *really brown* people, to prove that the sun is a permanent fixture and not just a dream, and next, a most important factor, is a quantity of people who are whiter and fatter than you are. So, to make yourself feel *really* good on your first day, enjoy that sunshine, relax as you feel the rays sink into your skin...and hang around someone who looks worse than you.

Not only does this give your morale a quick boost, but it also means you're going to feel less worried about exposing your carefully hidden flesh to the rest of the world. That is, until you're walking back to your apartment passing the poolside bar and somebody shouts out, '*Look...here come de WHITE FOLK!...*'

I wonder if she's hanging around ME to make HER feel better?

CHAPTER FIVE

Slap it on, suck it in and cover it up...

Eventually the time will come when your flesh is about to make its first major appearance in daylight since this time last year. You've done all you can to avoid it so far, by going to the Reps' meeting, rearranging all the furniture in your apartment and all the cosmetics on the bathroom shelf. But there's no avoiding that ego-shattering moment when you're in front of that cruel, full-length mirror wearing nothing but a pained expression, holding a tube of suncream and trying to suck your stomach in as far as it will go. (Which doesn't seem to be very far at all.) A suntan is but a trip to the pool away. But *what* a trip!

There is a temptation at this stage to keep your swimsuit or your shorts on all holiday, because you don't want to expose your hated bits to the world. Unfortunately this means that the worst bits will remain lily-white whilst the rest of you gets tanned, making them look a hundred times worse than before. So it *is* worth persevering.

TIPS FOR RELUCTANT STRIPPERS

- Put your lotion on in your apartment, where it's private.
- Sunblock all the embarrassing bits (e.g. nipples), and any places where you'll have to bend over, which no one wants to do half-naked in public if they can help it.
- Put on a bikini – yes, *a bikini* – a sarong, and a button-up top, which can be easily removed whilst lying down.
- Wait by the door until you feel the coast is clear and...run!

Then all that's left is to get settled, get out your book, your headphones, whatever...lie down, undo your buttons...shut your eyes, and you're off! No worries until it's time to turn over. No worries, that is, unless your sunbathing follows the same pattern as mine...

Arrive at sunbed. Put down towel. Wind blows it off. Pick up towel, put straight down, lie on it immediately. Realise have forgotten to sunblock nose. Sit up, search in bag for sunblock. Apply to face, wipe hands. Lie down again. Put on personal stereo. It switches off – the end of one side. Sit up again and change tape over. Lie down, take off bikini top. Relax. Wind blows towel onto legs. Sit up to remove towel and hat flies off. Search for bikini top. Find it, struggle to put it on whilst sucking in stomach. Can't do it up as it's twisted at the back. Take it off, finally do it up as someone's husband brings your hat back. You wonder why he's got that smirk on his face, then realise you have one breast poking out. Thank him kindly, lie down and wish you were dead...

Gradually, as you get used to lying about half-naked you should begin to realise that even the thinnest women have flabby bits or unsightly stretchmarks and you should hopefully start to feel a lot better about yourself. Once the initial pink blotches even out as you begin to turn from red to brown, you might even start *sitting up* in your bikini. If you're still racked with insecurity, then make sure you never go anywhere near the thinnest, most attractive people, and keep a good hold on that sarong whenever you stand up!

Once you're settled on your sunlounger you can have a good nose around you. Anyone looking really brown will be going home soon – thankfully. If you like to get talking to other people on holiday, watch to see who you might want to get to know, and whether they speak or are English, so that when you start to talk to them, they can talk back.

GOOD TIMES TO GET TALKING

- Walking about with children.
- Getting into the pool.
- Sitting by the pool with only your feet in because the water's too cold.
- Buying drinks at the bar.

BAD TIMES

- As you remove your child's ice cream from someone's stomach.
- As you remove your child's wet ball from someone's stomach.
- When someone has just taken her bikini top off.
- When someone has obviously just had a row.

BY THE POOL CHECKLIST

Is there:

- A man walking with his child pretending not to look at your nipples?
- A man in sunglasses who thinks you can't see his eyes, but you can...and they're looking at your nipples?
- Waiters from the bar walking very slowly past you?
- A wet football about to land on your stomach/book/ knock over your drink?
- A lot of men in awful swimming trunks?
- Europop musak coming from the bar?
- Lots and lots of children?
- A lot of women with really hairy armpits?
- Flies round your crotch? (Surely it's not just me...)
- Men causing havoc and showing off...

Men are curious beings on holiday. Some are incapable of sitting still for more than a couple of minutes and just have to keep getting up and showing off. This usually means that no one else can use the pool because they will be playing water polo and taking up all the room. Either that, or they will just hurl themselves in from as high a place as possible, regardless of whether anyone else is in there, and when they swim, they can't enjoy themselves unless they're splashing about, taking half the pool with them. Once we had a set of men who took snorkels into the pool and swam around banging into us and glaring as if we should have been fitted with a radar.

When men are not doing one of the above, they're parading around, rubbing their stomachs and sucking them in whilst trying not to slip on their flip-flops,

74

desperate to scratch their crotch as usual, but aware that they may have an audience. Normally the only time they'll be quiet and still is when the children demand attention and want to be taken for a long walk or play a game…and then, wouldn't you know it, they fall asleep…

There are a few men who are model parents and can lie quietly, swim without turning into maniacs and sit amongst half-naked women without their eyeballs popping out…but they really are few and far between, and they're normally with their wife or partner. The worst type of men are those in groups, out without a police escort on the hunt for anything remotely female and breathing, who spend all night drinking themselves stupid and trying to perfect their chat-up lines, and all day asleep with a hangover…so they practically never see the sun and might just as well have stayed at home.

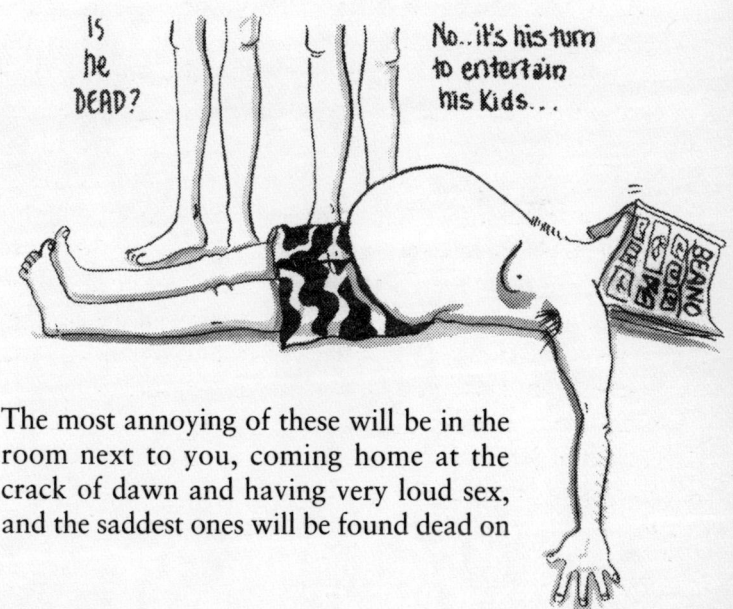

The most annoying of these will be in the room next to you, coming home at the crack of dawn and having very loud sex, and the saddest ones will be found dead on the beach because they fell asleep drunk and dehydrated. At least it gives you an excuse to go round poking them with sticks, 'Just testing to see if you were still alive...'

HOLIDAY ETIQUETTE

I am a fan of the pool rather than the beach, because there's less chance of having every orifice filled with sand after one gust of wind. The best pool areas will have a children's pool, which isn't just because it means I don't have to listen to them all day, but also it's actually better for the children. They can hurl themselves

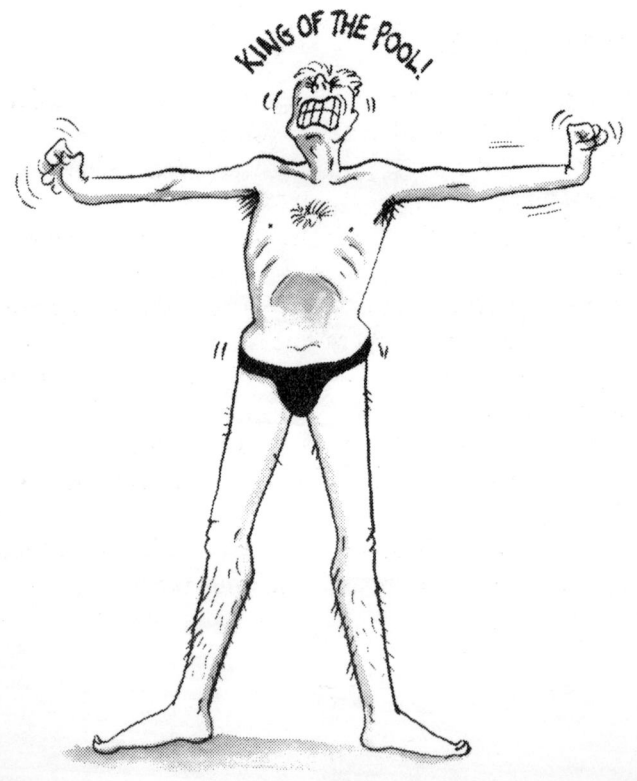

about, splash each other stupid, and no one will moan at them for drowning everyone in sight. It does also mean, of course, that the rest of us can swim happily in the pool without fear of being killed as their Lilos land on top of our heads. It's then just the men we have to watch out for.

Unfortunately it's not just children who can shatter your peace round the pool. You could get a Family From Hell, who arrive on their first day and bellow '*INNIT QUIET HERE?*' and sit in their enormous group, transforming the whole place in two minutes from a peaceful haven of sunworshipping bliss, to a cross between the terraces of Millwall and Dante's *Inferno*. So I believe there ought to be a general rule of pool etiquette that we all stick to…

BAD POOL ETIQUETTE

- Being a Bloke and eyeballing other women's nipples because your wife keeps her top on.
- Being a Bloke and eyeballing them even when your wife doesn't.
- Being a Bloke who takes the pool over and makes a lot of noise just because he's bored.
- Hurling yourself in the water without checking to see if there's anyone in there under you.
- Kneeling in the water and telling friends to jump in as it's really deep.
- Saying the water's lovely and warm, without adding, 'Only when you've been in an hour…' (Okay, that's funny.)
- Letting your children scream like madmen and not liking it when we sit over you and scream back.

VERY BAD POOL ETIQUETTE

- Letting your child wee in the pool.
- Having a ghetto blaster and blasting it.
- Having a camcorder and taking shots of topless women without offering a screen fee.
- Reserving your sunlounger early in the morning and not coming back all day.
- Being incredibly slim and showing off.
- Taking binoculars with you.
- Sitting by the pool taking notes and writing a book...

THE WORST POOL ETIQUETTE

- The British Caravan Syndrome...a predominantly British peculiarity, which not only happens by the pool, but in cafés and cinemas and...you guessed it...caravan sites. If there's one person in the whole pool area/café/cinema/caravan site...the British will go and park right next to them. Not one or two seats or spaces away, but *right* next to them. Don't ask me why it's a British thing, it's just something I've

DAY ONE

DAY TWO

RESERVED!

DAY THREE

KEEP OFF!

I SAW IT FIRST

DAY FOUR

SUPERMERCADO

noticed over the years, a complete disregard for personal space. It's especially annoying on holiday, because nothing makes you more nervous than having total strangers parking themselves right next to you when you've got hardly any clothes on!

I mentioned it briefly earlier, now let's investigate the Great Sunlounger Debate. To Reserve...or *NOT* to Reserve? That is the question. It isn't an exclusively German obsession to be down the pool at the crack of dawn superglueing your towel to the one sunlounger that doesn't collapse when you sit on it. Lots of people do it. Mainly when they realise that if they don't do it too, they'll have to camp out overnight or end up on a towel on the floor, which they'll have to share with the local wildlife whilst being trampled to death by racing children.

Some resorts have a 'No-Reserving' policy, which can work, unless the staff don't care because they have the sunshine all year long and it gives them something to laugh at. There was a Family From Hell one year who never reserved any sunloungers, they just waited until people went to the loo and then pinched them. They were an especially tattooed crew and it was hard to imagine them being reasonable about it. Some people take great macho pride in hurling other people's towels in the pool just because they got up earlier than them, and it can actually start rows. Over a *sunlounger*? On your *holidays*?

This isn't so much of a problem if you spend your holiday on the beach. There's nothing quite like hearing the sound of the sea as you lie in the sun, and the sensation of warm sand between your toes. In your clothes, in your hair, in your pants...

BEACH PLUSES

- The sea is just a walk away.
- You *really* feel like you're on holiday.
- Nothing beats a swim in the sea.
- You get LIFEGUARDS.

BEACH DOWNERS

- You get covered in sand.
- Sea salt dries your skin when you swim.
- You don't know what else as well as salt is in the sea.

- The local animals roam free, and you could be lying on their favourite toilet, or one could take a fancy to your legs and sit on them.
- There's always some slim tart showing off by standing up and rubbing her suncream on her nipples before playing topless volleyball.
- Just when you're dropping off, having found a quiet place to go topless, you open your eyes hours later to find a café has opened up and you're the entertainment.
- There aren't many toilets handy...so where do people go?

POOL PLUSES

- You don't have to be an expert to go swimming and when you do get out of your depth you can cling to the sides, whereas the sea hasn't got any sides.
- You don't get covered in sand.

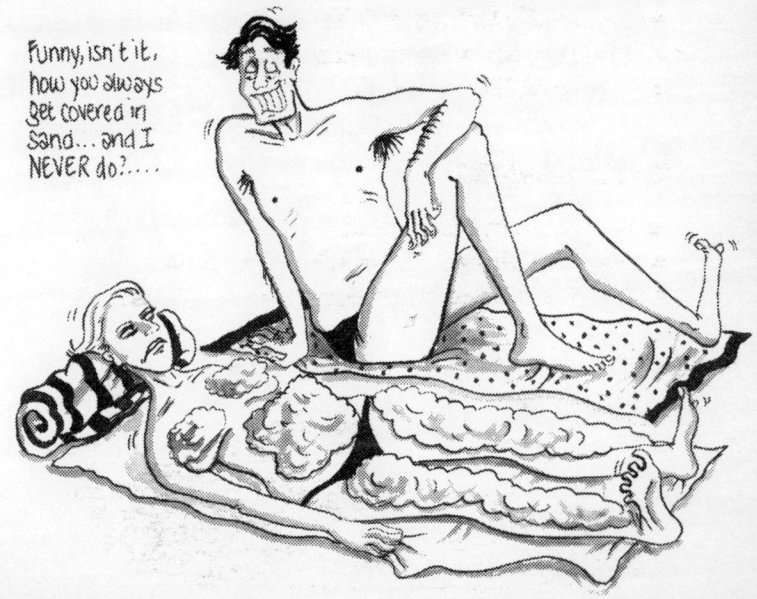

Funny, isn't it, how you always get covered in sand... and I NEVER do?....

- Facilities are within easy reach.
- It's handy for your apartment and a shorter distance to walk about in your swimsuit...

POOL DOWNERS

- You miss the sound of the sea.
- You can't build sandcastles.
- Waiters and workmen hover about all day.
- You can't escape the Reps, who try to get you to kill yourself by doing aerobics in the midday heat.

No matter where you go, you have to be aware of how long you're in the sun, how often you have to apply that suncream, and which bits of you are getting exposed the most. Here's a guide for SAFE AND SENSIBLE SUNNING...

STRAP MARKS

- Remember that Rod Stewart song, 'The First Cut Is The Deepest'? Well, as far as sunbathing goes, the first marks last the longest! So, boob tubes on from the start if you don't want your chest to look like an ordnance survey map after a couple of days.

YOU GET WHITE MARKS WHEN

- You go for a walk in a strappy top or your swimsuit.
- You keep your swimsuit on all the time.
- You sit up in a bikini reading a book and your stomach creases.

- You have big bosoms.
- Your bottom is saggy. (Sorry, fact of life...)

WATCH OUT FOR

- Having a really brown front and back...and lily-white sides.
- That annoying bit of neck that never seems to get brown.
- Labels on your swimwear that stick up, making ridiculous white marks.

BITS THAT BURN

- Normally areas where the skin is thinnest and therefore vulnerable: Collarbone, Shoulders, Soles Of

Should've worn a BOOB TUBE...

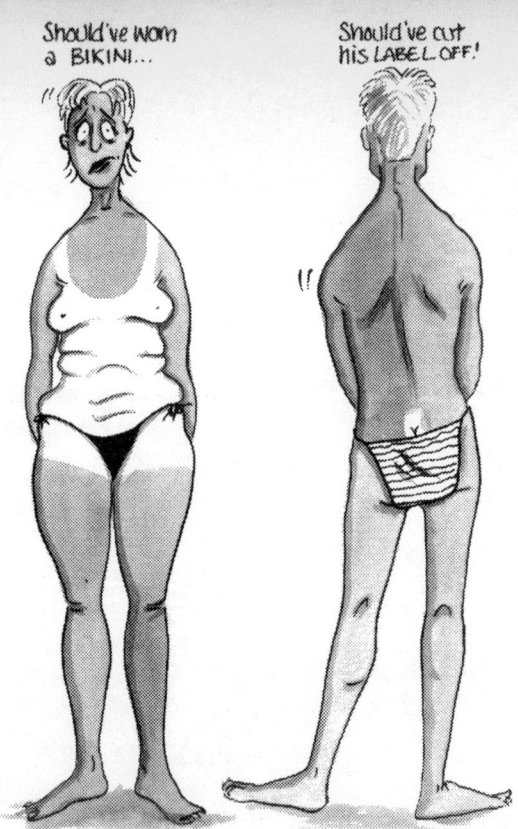

Feet, Breast Bone, Backs Of Knees (although saying that, I have singed my bottom before, not, unfortunately because the skin was thin and near to the bone, but because when I lay on my front it was the nearest thing to the sun...)

- Also areas that get exposed all the time that you may forget about: Forehead, Nose, Instep...The nose is always the first thing to peel and can look like a bad case of eczema...so slap on sunblock when you're not sunbathing, so you limit the amount of sun it gets.

How To Avoid The Burn

- Always use cream, not oil. Remember that oil is used for frying, and you'll never use it again.
- Start off with a higher factor cream for the first few days so your skin gets used to the sun, and a lower one when you feel your skin can take it.
- If you're unlucky enough to love the sun and be incredibly pale-skinned, keep slapping on that high factor cream and cover yourself up when you're out walking. Always take a hat, and wear it!

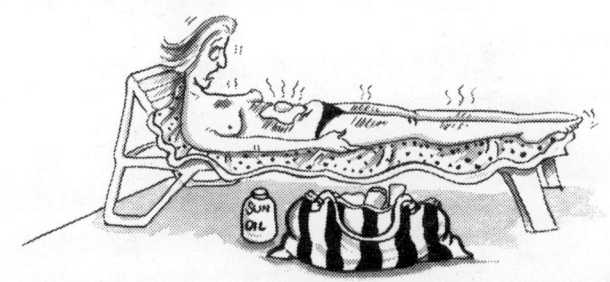

If You Do Burn

- Take it easy until you feel less sore.
- Sunblock the sensitive spots, as it not only stops you from burning any more, it also keeps you cooler.
- Take that large T-shirt out of the case, and use it to cover up the burnt areas so you can carry on with the rest of your body.
- Remember that the towels provided are usually quite rough, and drying yourself with them can feel like you're using a cheese grater...so take a soft one, just in case. (Only don't put it on a sunlounger, or you may never see it again...)

How To Keep The Burn Cool

- Sunblock, as I said, and one of those new 'cooling gels' which promise to keep the burn at bay.
- You can put your moisturiser in the fridge, which can be very soothing when your legs are radiating more heat than Sellafield, although there are side effects of combining intensive heat and moisturiser. You could wake up to find you're welded to the sheets...
- Obviously the best way to keep cool is to do all the above and get a loved one to sit over you with a fan...only make sure they don't get distracted or bored, because they could end up giving you a bit of a scrape, which is the *last* thing you need...

How To Keep That Tan...

You've gone to an awful lot of trouble and expense to get this tan. You may have even suffered considerable discomfort...so you might as well try to hang on to it for as long as you can. There's nothing worse than having a really big peel the day before you go home, so you feel like you've lost most of your colour by the time you get there. The less you burn, the less you'll peel, and if you use shower and bath stuff that has added moisturisers, your skin will stay good and soft. If you do peel, keep slapping on the suncream and the moisturiser. Rolling round on the floor, trying to stick it back on, will *not* work...

SAFEST SUNBATHING

CHAPTER SIX

Can I *wee* in this pool, Dad?

(A look at parents and children on holiday...)

If you haven't already gathered, I'm not a parent, and therefore have not got an automatic switch-off system that blocks out ear-piercing squeals, or an automatic smile that instantly flashes when someone's child throws a bucket of water over my favourite book, or hurls half the beach in my face. I don't actually object to being surrounded by children (much); it's just that I wish I wasn't expected to turn into a child minder or a free entertainer just because I'm single, or to have to pretend I'm enjoying myself whilst my eardrums are bleeding.

In an ideal world, holiday resorts would lump all the families together at one end of the complex, like one huge mothers and toddlers group. That way I would have less chance of being woken up by the sound of Baby trying on Mummy's shoes (clickclackclick-clackclickclackclickclack), or toddler getting up and running to his parents' room at five every morning (thudthudthudthudthud. CRASH! *Waaaaaaaaah*!)

The best way to avoid children en masse is to go away in term time, watching out for any half terms and bank holidays. This

doesn't let you off completely, because thanks to airlines letting babies travel for free, there are bound to be hoards of women who look like they've gone straight from the maternity ward and onto the plane. Consequently, your holiday will ring with the cries of breast-hungry babies, which means you have to turn up your personal stereo, but which is infinitely better than being surrounded by breast-hungry teenage boys who hang around dribbling over your nipples and using you as part of their sex education project.

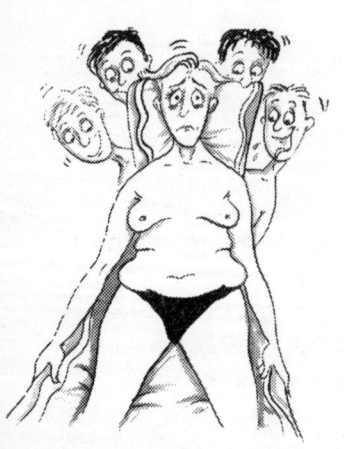

How To Spot The Parents

Apart from the fact that they're the ones with the babies, you can always spot them because the bags under their eyes are almost as big as the ones they're carrying, they look like they haven't had time to do their hair since the baby was born, and they have uneven suntan marks from chasing baby round the pool all day.

Types Of Parents
(All spotted on different holidays)

- Those who let their children run wild so they don't interfere with their holiday.
- Those who sit with their backs to their children, and every now and again mumble, 'Don't do that, Holly!' just in case Holly's doing anything. Holly is, in fact, tottering on the edge of the pool and is starting to lean over. Everyone else has to instantly become a Nanny and try to steer her away. (Except me. I'm making bets on how long it takes before Holly falls in...)
- Parents who sit at the pool bar all day and never play with their children or change their shorts.
- Parents who tell their children total crap in order to stop them from doing anything, e.g. 'Don't touch that, it's poisonous'...'Don't stroke that kitten, it's got rabies'...and, 'That man's a policeman and he'll arrest you if you pick your nose again.'
- The 'thwack-a-minute' parents, whose children always seem to be the ones who least deserve it.
- Parents who feed their children chocolates and chips

all day to keep them quiet, and when they're being sick all night, blame it on foreign food.

- The 'don't you criticise MY child' parents, as their child steals other childrens' toys, cheats at games and tries to be King Of The Pool by drowning every other child around.
- The 'one-upmanship' parents, whose child has the biggest inflatable in the pool, the most toys, and whose sandcastles are architectural marvels, with twenty turrets, bridges, landscape gardening and a hand-painted national flag.

DADS ON HOLIDAY

Now, on holiday, kids desperately want their dads to be brilliant at everything. As soon as he dons his shorts, it's an unwritten law that he's got to be an Olympic athlete, a conjurer and a stand-up comedian. More often than not, he's almost as miserable and reluctant to do anything as he is at home, and he might even turn out to be a CRAP DAD.

HOW TO SPOT A CRAP DAD
(All spotted on one holiday)

- He doesn't have much to do with the kids for the rest of the year, so he tries to make up for it by trying to play loads of games...only he doesn't know which ones they like...
- He has absolutely no authority, so he tries to keep them amused by buying loads of new toys and chasing round like a madman.

CRAP DAD

- The King of Crap Dads won't move to catch a ball (he's lighting his fag), he won't run about or play football (he's overweight, can't run and might drop his fag), and he'll never, *never*, go in the water (it's too cold...and it'll put his fag out).
- The King Of Crap Dads' sandcastle is a pathetic crumbling mound with only one turret and a fag end for a flag.

When there are teenagers about the best entertainment you can get is watching to see how their parents embarrass them...

- Their dad is in really gaudy shorts and a tropical shirt.
- Their mum stops wearing her bra. ('Oh, *MUM!* Your nipples are showing again!')
- Best of all, is when their mother decides to go top-less. Then you can't see them for dust. It only works with teenagers, of course, as babies just think it's lunchtime...

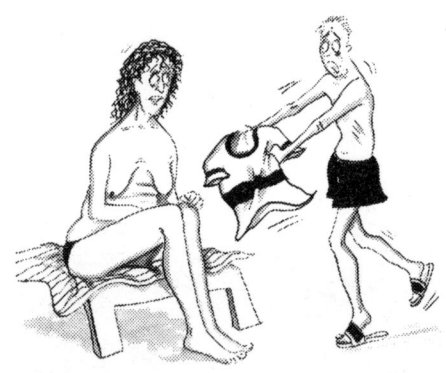

CHILDREN IN THE POOL

Not only are children likely to completely take over the pool by leaping in on top of you in huge numbers, but they also use it as an arena where they show up any adults that aren't as good at diving, treading water and swimming underwater for ages as they are. They're doing double back-flip somersaults whilst you cling to the steps at the shallow end. The most dangerous time to be in the pool is at the same time as a child who is desperately trying to impress a Crap Dad. There's no knowing what they'll do to drag his attention away from his pint and his fag and his game of pool.

The worst thing about children and pools is that they tend to regard it as one large toilet, which is why I'm all in favour of them having a pool of their own to do it in. I remember sitting by the pool as a family of new arrivals were exploring the area. When they got to the pool, one of the children actually said, 'Can I wee in this pool, Dad?', to which we all hurled ourselves in to get as much swimming done as possible before he started.

HOW TO SURVIVE CHILDREN ON HOLIDAY

- Find out where the children's pool is, and keep well clear.
- Make sure you have VERY loud music on your head-phones.
- Try not to make eye contact, or else they'll think you like them and want to play.
- Have a child yourself and enjoy terrorising anyone who looks like they're getting a better suntan than you are.

CHAPTER SEVEN

Wine, waiters, walkabouts... and ways to pass the time...

People tend to develop different routines when they're on holiday. Some hit the pool the minute the sun comes up, and others use the cooler mornings to walk about, explore, and have a good nose at fellow tourists...I am one of the latter; as long as the weather stays hot all afternoon, I like to spend my mornings in a café by the sea, indulging in a spot of People-Watching. Most of us end up doing this, because once you've stopped gazing out to sea, there's not much left to look at.

PEOPLE-WATCHING CHECKLIST

Spot The...New Arrivals

- They're tired.
- They're hunting for the *supermercado*, or else are laden down with shopping on their way back.

- They're PALE.
- They're still wearing their vests under their shirts, or their bras under their suntops.
- They're being chased by timeshare touts.

Spot The...Foreigner

- They'll be carrying a foreign paper.
- They're natural blondes.
- They have something in English on their T-shirts that makes absolutely no sense at all, such as: 'Gin Tonic Gin Tonic'; 'Hello Surf'; 'This Means The Jeans'...
- If they're German, the men will have really naff haircuts (short on top with a long thin pigtail) and either a crap, weedy moustache or a huge handlebar 'Village People' number.
- If they're locals, they'll be hairy, tanned, and watching *you*.

Spot The...British

- We only speak English.
- Our men have the most tattoos.
- We order chips with everything.

General Things To Spot

- Men who only ever wear shorts on holiday, who choose garish colours and ghastly patterns and who look like they'd really like to get their suits back on.
- Men who just can't tear themselves away from their ankle socks and who wear them with their flip-flops.
- People in T-shirts that tell you where they went last year...or ten years ago.
- Holiday haircuts. (They're too short.)
- Holiday perms. (They're too frizzy.)
- Holiday hi-lites. (They're too dry, and after a week the hair looks like it's going to drop out.)

Evening Spotting

- Men showing off their muscles.
- Women showing off their midriffs.
- Women in strappy sandals who thought all the paths would be finished this year.
- People who didn't bring their jackets and are freezing to death in the evening breeze.
- People with children who should have been in bed an hour ago.
- People trying to suck in their stomachs when they haven't been to the toilet for a week and have just finished a huge paella.

One of the biggest pleasures about being somewhere warm is being able to eat outside. At home, restaurants shove a couple of plastic seats on the path next to a major road three times a year and we think that's really living. On holiday the worst thing that will happen will be that you have to share your table with mosquitos or a few stray dogs who come and plonk their heads on the table and blow their nose on your food.

Another pleasure about eating abroad is the experience of seeing waiters do the job properly. None of this, '*I'm really an actor, you know...*' crap we get at home. These boys take it seriously and they do it with style. They are also terrible flirts, which, if handled properly, can be used in your favour...

DIFFERENT TYPES OF WAITERS

- Those who ask your nipples what they'd like to drink.

- Those who will try to have sex with you because the local girls won't have sex with them.
- Those who think that all British women are easy because an awful lot have been.
- Those who like you to come to their restaurant, enjoy a good flirt, and then think themselves lucky they're not married to you because you're far too independent.

HOW TO HANDLE WAITERS

- Be blonde. If you can't be blonde, be pleasant.
- Attempt to speak a few phrases in their language. At least 'Hello' and 'Thank you'. (Also learn 'No' and 'I'm married' – just in case.)

- Every now and again get the cleavage out, especially near the end of your holiday when your money is running out, as it can get you a free cocktail, extra brandies, or even a free meal if you've been working on the rapport from day one. (If you're there as an unaccompanied female, make sure you know exactly *which* perks you're being offered...)

WHAT NOT TO DO

- DON'T do that annoying British Imperial thing of shouting at them when they don't understand you.
- DON'T click your fingers and shout '*OY-MANUEL!*', because you think it's funny.
- DON'T always have chips. At least *try* some of the local food.
- Don't overdo the flirting if you're out of practice, and don't think they're madly in love with you when you do flirt, and it works.

YOU KNOW YOU CAN HANDLE THEM WHEN

- You've had at least one free drink, with added sparklers.
- They save you the best table when you go in.
- They let you off speaking the language and always speak to you in English.
- They give some perks to your partner.

You'll probably notice that the drinks are much bigger here than they are at home, and if you hadn't noticed, maybe it will account for all those hangovers. I've had some wines on holiday that make paint stripper look appetising, and red wine is especially lethal, so maybe you should stick to beers and spirits, bearing in mind that their single measure is equivalent to our triple.

There could be an advantage to having huge drinks. It makes the entertainment more bearable. If you're not the 'nite'-clubbing type, or have small children to look after, you'll probably find yourself one night stuck in the bar with the likes of 'Jimmy Guitar' and his Eric Clapton impressions, or the lone organ player who sings, 'I jes called to say I lav you...and I mean it from the *boredom* of my heart...' The reps often take it upon themselves to turn into Redcoats and organise competitions and games just in case the last thing on your mind was a quiet drink. Other entertainment could be sitting on your patio with a bottle of local wine, playing strip Scrabble; you could sit next to the Holiday Bore and see how long it takes before you hit him, or you could set up a book on how late the couple next door will start to have sex later on.

The best entertainment has to be trying to guess when the maid is coming...

MOST FREQUENT TIMES

- When you're asleep.
- When you've just gone to the toilet and the bathroom door is open.
- When you're naked.

No matter how hard you try to anticipate her arrival you will find that it's always too late. She does that trick of ringing the bell once, and before you've had the chance to draw breath to say, 'No', she's got the key in the door and is in, catching you hopping about with one leg in your pants. In general, most maids tend to be very pleasant, and it can't be a very agreeable job, clearing up after tourists.

There are some, however, who are real dragons, who glare at you and tut if you haven't washed up yet, and growl to make you lift up your feet whilst they mop, which is a bit too much like having your mother round. I always start the holiday by clearing up and making the bed before the maid comes so she doesn't think I'm a slob, but not being a fan of housework at the best of times, never mind on my holidays, it never lasts long. Gradually the beds stop being made, clothes are left lying about and I start to leave the washing up in the sink. (Well, you can hope...)

CHAPTER EIGHT

Friends, friction and fornication...

When you're on holiday you're involved in various relationships: you and your partner (with or without children), with friends, meeting people when you're there...and of course the Holiday Romance...

WHEN IT'S YOU AND YOUR PARTNER, 24 HOURS A DAY

The worst aspect of going away with your loved one is that you're probably not used to being on your own with him all day and all night. You can't get excited about your next date, look forward to seeing him after being out at work all day, or listening for the sound of his key in the door...because he's already there. All the time, wherever you look, and if you're not careful, it's a recipe for disaster.

GENERAL ARGUMENTS

- Eyeing up other womens' nipples.
- Over-flirting with the waiters.
- Not wanting to go anywhere.
- Not wanting to do anything.

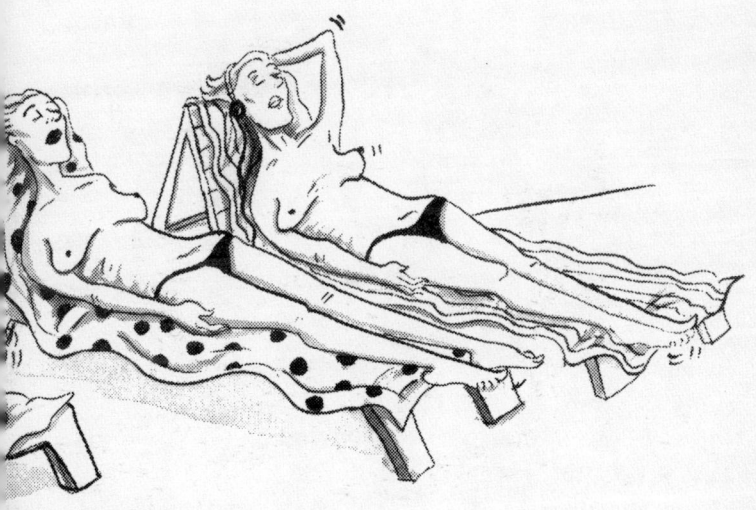

Most people like a change when they go on holiday, a change of scenery, a change of weather, a change of diet...but some undergo a dramatic *personality* change the minute they get off the plane. Executives and people who have to make decisions all day at work refuse to do anything on holiday. Independent career women turn into gibbering girlie wrecks at the thought of flying or ordering a meal in a foreign language. You could go away with someone who you thought was adventurous and game for anything, but who turns into a complete coward who doesn't *want* to go out into the country-side in the dark, thank you very much, even if there *is* a nice little taverna somewhere...

HOW TO HAVE AN ALMOST PERFECT HOLIDAY TOGETHER

- Make sure you have some time on your own, even if it is just sticking your headphones on for a while.
- Share any duties, like making the tea in the morning, and especially any cooking.
- Be flexible. If your partner doesn't like sitting by the pool all the time, give up a day and do what he wants. Or else don't moan at him when he wants to do it by himself.

GOING AWAY WITH FRIENDS

It sounds like a great idea, to spend your holidays with some of your best and dearest friends. But this again can turn into a disaster, and you could end up hating each other after a week...

The best way to arrange it is to be completely sure

before you go about what sort of holiday you all want, so those who want to blob by the pool all day can do so without being pressured into going on jeep rides or water ski-ing, and those who want to do that won't sit around by the pool feeling bored. It's also a good idea not to spend all day every day together, so arrange to be apart at some point each day, or else you'll have nothing to talk about.

MAKING FRIENDS WHILST YOU'RE THERE

If you're on holiday with a partner, a few new faces can prevent you from getting tired of your old one. You may find that you've already started having mini-conversations with people on the plane, the coach or by the pool...if talking to people when they're half-naked

doesn't bother you. There will be a night in a bar when you get tempted to spend an evening with them because you're starting to get fed up with talking to the same person all the time, but WATCH OUT in case the only thing you have in common with them is slagging off the Reps and talking about the weather. Otherwise you could spend all your precious holiday time in the company of people you can't stand. (In this instance, make sure you don't swop addresses, or if you do, give a false one.)

WATCH OUT also for the HOLIDAY BORE. Every resort has at least one. Usually it's a bloke who's over thirty-five and travelling with his mother because no one else will go with him, or else he's with his very weary looking family, who have heard all his bad jokes and his anecdotes too many times before. He'll introduce himself to everyone, find out your name and keep

calling you by it; he's not happy unless he's told you all about his hobbies, his job and his life story, what kind of car he's got, and he'll do his best to buy you a drink so he can sit at your table and not budge all night. You'll spot him because he shakes hands with everyone and superglues himself to anyone who's too shy or too polite to sock him in the mouth. Either that, or you'll guess who he is when everyone starts running when they see him coming...

HOLIDAY ROMANCES

The sun is shining, you're on your holidays, you've started to get a suntan; what could be a better combination for making a complete fool of yourself? Even the most undesirable, badly dressed, over-fed moron can start to look half decent when he's got a suntan and you've had a skinful – so watch it!

Romance can start as early as the airport, if you're in the holiday mood and the love-radar is on. Do try and hold on until you get there, as it *is* a bit desperate to fall for someone in the first few hours...

When you're on an 18-30 holiday, romance isn't exactly on the menu. Most people are there to meet the opposite sex and have some. As much as possible and as varied as possible. The quietest, most unassuming people turn into irresponsible sex-mad hounds as soon as they hit foreign soil. Whether it's with fellow Brits or sexy Spaniards, all good intentions for Safe Sex fly out of the window and the condoms remain in the suitcase. Now, just because he comes from dear old Britain doesn't mean he's free from all known germs, and the Spaniard might well look even better out of his tight black trousers than he does in them, but that's no excuse either. If he's doing it with you now, you can guarantee he's done it with someone else before you arrived and will do it with another one when you've gone. So don't kid yourself AND GET THOSE CONDOMS OUT!

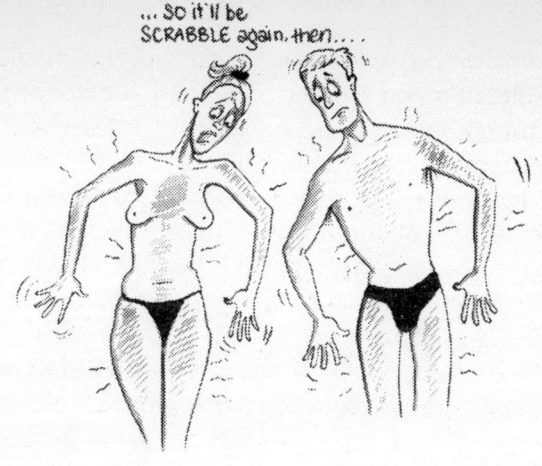

The best holiday romances are those you have when you're still young enough to be with your parents, you're under strict supervision and all you get to do is have long lingering glances and a couple of snogs. These romances you always remember with fondness and few regrets. Unlike most you have when you're older...

When you're on holiday with the person you live with, you probably won't get much in the way of romance, and if you've got children or sunburn you won't be getting much in the way of sex either...

SEX ON HOLIDAY

Like birthdays, Christmas and Saturday nights, holidays are a time when you're expected to have an awful lot of sex, because you're together all the time and there's not much else to do. Unfortunately many elements can come into play that stop you from having any play at all.

THINGS THAT PUT YOU OFF SEX

- Too much sangria.
- Too much poison paella.
- Too many rows.
- Too many children.
- Too much SUNBURN.
- Too many sudden attacks by kamikaze mosquitos.

If you have the inclination but very singed skin, then you'll have to work a little harder and find a position

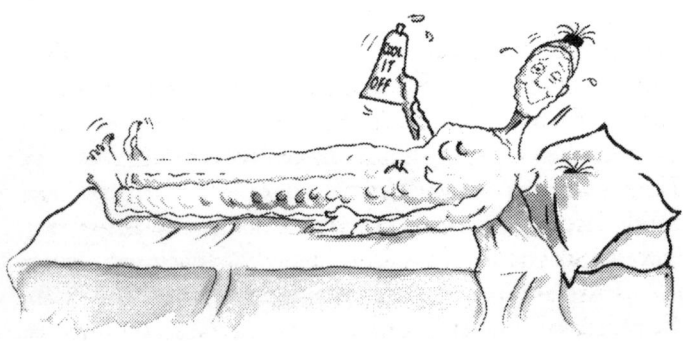

where you don't actually touch much. (Good exercise for the arm muscles, but you may eventually find it's too much trouble and give up.) You can ease the burn by rubbing in each other's moisturiser and see where that gets you, or jump in a freezing cold shower. If you find it's just too painful and decide not to bother at all, make sure that you're very, very nice to each other instead. If you *do* manage to have stress-free, burn-free sex, try and make sure it's with the person you came with...

CHAPTER NINE

The last tube of suncream...

You're nice and brown, you're feeling relaxed, you're really starting to enjoy yourself and getting into the swing of your holiday. Then you realise you haven't got much money left and tomorrow is your LAST DAY! Panic will now set in, especially if you've just started to peel or are convinced that you're getting *lighter*. So instead of visiting the old village or the port like you said you would, you decide to spend *all* of your last day by the pool or on the beach, despite the fact that the sun looks like it's deserted you and you're almost out of suncream.

LAST DAY CHECKLIST

- Have you got enough money left for a couple more meals?
- Have you kept some spare in case you're delayed at the airport?
- Are you still talking to your husband/partner/ friends?
- Do you still like your children?

You will find that the approach of your last day, for some strange reason, fills you with an urge to hang on to the memory of all that sunshine, and buy a souvenir to take home, even if it is just a plastic bull or a flamenco dancer made out of old toilet rolls and covered in shells. You will also discover just how stingy you really are when it comes to buying duty-frees for the family. Their value diminishes rapidly depending on

how much money you've got left. A large bottle of *Johnny Walker* for your dad can quickly turn into a small carafe of *Pedro's Plonk* if you're strapped for cash, and you take it on yourself to decide who's giving up smoking if it boils down to a choice between a huge packet of fags for them and an extra jug of sangria for you. If you are still attached to people who you've discovered you have nothing in common with but who won't get the hint and go away, you may by now be plotting their deaths or working out plans for how you can escape from them for one last day. You should also be starting to hunt down your Rep to make sure your flight hasn't been changed again and you've only got half an hour to pack. There should be a timetable in reception that tells you which days your Rep will be available for you. Or rather, which days they'll pop their head round the corner, have a quick look round and then run away before anyone asks them to do something tricky. Like help them.

Find out which time you have to leave your apartment, what time you're being taken to the airport and how many hours you'll have to kill in between. Over the years I've noticed that most resorts turn into old-fashioned landladies when it comes to evacuating your rooms, and insist that you leave at midday, whether your flight is at three in the afternoon or ten at night. One year I was struck down by a poison pizza and wasn't allowed to stay in my nice, familiar bathroom. Instead I had to occupy one of the *two* apartments they left for the *forty* or so families who were going home that day and would need them to shower in. Unfortunately my occupancy meant that they now only had one, and no Rep was to be found to solve the situation. Consequently as I was flying home trying not to inhale the food or watch anyone eat, others were emptying sand from their clothes and trying to wash in the toilets.

The weather on your last day must be either torrential rain so you won't mind going home, or one last blast of sunshine to keep your tan up. The best thing to do is to get as much as possible sorted and packed the night before, so your memories are of holidays and not laundry. You'll have enough of that to look at when you get home. It's a good idea to have something warmer to wear for when you get off the plane, especially if you arrive in the middle of the night and have to wait for a train. Roll up a pair of leggings and a top in your hand luggage and change on the plane or at the airport. Look on your balcony or patio so you don't leave any drying swimwear behind, and check under the bed for stray pants.

As you leave the apartment, remember to leave a tip for the maid, especially if she's been pleasant, and she could probably do with it. Most people sort through their coins (which you can rarely change when you get home) and at least that *looks* like you've been generous. Try not to get unnecessarily critical by keeping a list of all the times you thought she didn't use enough elbow grease or skimped on the toilet duck. You may feel she's already had quite enough perks catching you half-naked every day for a fortnight...

HOW TO SPOT PEOPLE ON THEIR LAST DAY

- Their clothes look neat and clean, and they're back in long sleeves.
- They're terrified of eating anything in case they spill it on their clean clothes and have to get the case open again.

- They're counting their mosquito bites.
- They aren't talking to each other.
- They're gazing wistfully at you as you go down to the beach.
- They're desperately checking the papers for weather reports in case all those thunderstorms they've been wishing on Britain are set to arrive the minute they land.

LAST DAY DON'TS

- DON'T overdo the sunbathing, as you might not get a chance to shower, and the seats are prickly enough when you're not burnt. They're like sitting on a bed of *razor blade*s when you are.
- DON'T eat anything you haven't tried before, because a plane isn't the best place to be when you're ill. Believe me.

- DON'T forget those warmer clothes for when you land.
- DON'T do a Shirley Valentine unless you're prepared and have most of your savings with you.
- DON'T expect Pedro to propose. He's probably hiding somewhere until you've gone and the next lot arrive.

Another annoying thing about leaving your room early, is that you have to leave your bags sitting in reception all day. There's probably not much chance of them getting stolen unless you're really unlucky, but there's always a chance that someone will do the caravan trick on you and plonk their bags right next to yours, which means that as they're going on a different plane to a different place, your bags may go off with them. So you'll have to display your labels prominently, and check on them every now and again. I shouldn't leave it up to the receptionist, as she probably has enough to do, and she may be a close friend of the maid who you only left fifty pesetas for.

Your Rep, Sammi, told you that the minibus will arrive, 'Basically at 14.45…that's a quarter to three. *OKAY?*' and you make sure you're there early so you don't hold everyone up. No danger of that, as Sammi is the one who's late. As the bus can't *possibly* go without her, you just have to sit and wait. Which you do a lot of on your way home, because even if you do get there early, the queue is always a mile long. Once Sammi's arrived, she ushers you all on to the bus as if it was you who were late. She can't *possibly* sit there without giving you her running commentary which goes along the lines of, 'Please make sure you have all your luggage with you', which is a bit pointless as you're already well on your way – courtesy of the driver who, as well

as being a complete madman on the road, doesn't appear to have ever used deodorant. And guess who's sitting in direct line with his armpits...

It's a smashing trip. Sammi drones on in tones that would make an insomniac drop off, the minibus is hurling you all out of your seats...and you're trying to find an air pocket somewhere that isn't filled with B.O.

You approach the airport, after passing all the places you meant to see but didn't, and wondering why there hasn't been a serial killer who targeted Reps, but that it can only be a matter of time, and Sammi says, 'We are now approaching the airport, *aeroporta*', just in case you missed all those great big signposts. You can see one queue that is so big that it's curling round the terminal and looks like it's halfway back to your resort, and yup...it's yours!

Whilst you're in the queue, have a look to see if you recognise anyone from the flight out, and if their suntan is better than yours. See if you can spot the Family From Hell working their way to the front of the queue, or being escorted out of the country by armed guards. Watch out for any ginger people who haven't looked after their skin properly and have burnt; they usually produce some spectacular blisters that can keep you amused for ages. You can tell anyone who's been on an 18-30 holiday, because of their very pale skin and lovebite splattered necks.

A good way to pass the time is to listen in on other people's conversations. This way you get to hear what other resorts were like and what other people thought of their Reps, which can save you getting any brochures next year, unless, that is, they are completely stupid, like the family who travelled with us in the minibus. They were having real old rant about the resort. Now, we went there because the brochure said it was quiet, not too touristy and not recommended for families because there weren't many facilities for children. These people complained because it was too quiet, there were no discos, and no water-parks for the kids. They went with the same company as us, they must have had the same brochure as us, so what parts were *they* reading?

Once you have spent most of your time in one queue only to have them open another one the minute you get to the front, and once you have discovered that you will be sitting between two total strangers all the way home, you can start to look around the airport and head for a café. Try to resist the temptation to go straight through to the departure lounge, as you might find that all the best places are in the rest of the building, and you could save yourself from having to sit on the floor because everyone else has had the same idea, which means you're all squashed together in the one place in the airport where the air conditioning isn't working, queueing up for yet another hour for a lukewarm coke and a cold coffee. So it pays to look round first.

THINGS YOU DON'T WANT TO SEE AT THIS AIRPORT

- A sign saying, 'Sorry, air conditioning broken.'
- A sign saying, 'Sorry, only one toilet working.'
- Any sign of bad weather as it means you'll be stuck in the airport all day until they decide you have to be put up in a hotel all night, only to go through it all again tomorrow...

Entertainment at this airport will be much the same as at home, and the butterflies (or, in my case, a herd of elephants) will be starting to charge around at the sight of all those planes again. So get the puzzle book out, as you can't possibly have anything left to say to your partner. And if your children are driving you to distraction and everyone else to the bar, you'll probably be tempted to do that old parental trick of pretending they're not yours. Much more productive and guaranteed to keep them quiet for ages is to send them off on a mission to see how much skin they can peel from people's legs under the tables.

If you haven't got a book to read, or you've read everything in sight, including the back of your coke can, you could play 'Spot who's the most burnt'…'Spot who's about to get divorced'…or 'Spot which children will be sick on the plane'. Most fun of all is 'Guess who's going to hold you up'. On the way over it was that hippy student, who probably spent the first half of his holiday wondering why the back of his head was so sore. Now who's it going to be? A gang of lads who have forgotten which day they're going home, a couple of girls who have fallen in love and are refusing to leave, or a Family From Hell who have started a fight with an airport official because he looked like he was smirking at their passport photo?

One year we were held up for ages by a truly moronic couple. Their names were called out over the Tannoy until we were sick of hearing them. The pilot said he'd hang on a bit in case they were in trouble. Then we heard stories about their being total pains in the neck all holiday, late for every trip, being the only ones who wanted a Eurovision Karaoke night, and forever calling out Reps in the middle of the night because their taps were too tight or for some equally weedy reason. Although I quite liked the idea of someone being able to make a Rep's life miserable, I didn't want it happening to me; and we were all getting good and twitchy, when they arrived at the front of the plane. They had to walk past most of us to get to their seats, and if that wasn't enough to show them up, they were both wearing T-shirts which said 'I'M WITH THIS IDIOT'…I kid you not…

CHAPTER TEN

If you've got it, flaunt it...

If the flight home hasn't got a film, you're well and truly stuffed, because you've read every book, listened to every tape and don't want to talk to your partner until you've been home at least a week. This is the time when you're most vulnerable to being lured into conversation with a bored fellow passenger. One year we approached our seats only to be greeted by a line of aged men, and when one of them, who thought he was a real wag, said, 'Ooh, I want the Dolly Bird next to me!'...I knew I was doomed.

It's amazing how many intimate, personal details you can learn about total strangers once you start talking to them. So don't. Unless you're interested in not only hearing about wonderful, talented offspring and developing house extensions, but seeing the *photos* too! If they're pensioners, you get the additional joy of an awful lot of hospital stories, which are great, especially when you're eating. By the end of the flight, if you last that long, you know the names of all their grandchildren, what they did in the War, and how many times they had to be cut up and prodded about before their gall bladder was fixed.

The plane begins its descent into dear old Blighty, and you can't wait to have the first cup of tea back in your own home. (But you'll have to if you didn't order any milk.) You look forward to seeing the house, to seeing the cat, to seeing the television…but most of all, to seeing one of your really *pale* friends.

You leave the plane, you smile at the stewardess so she has to stretch her mouth even further, and trot happily down the corridors to pick up your bags.

HOW YOU KNOW YOU'RE BACK IN BRITAIN

- The weather automatically starts to get worse.
- The first person you meet is either rude or bonkers.
- You find that tube of suncream you thought you'd lost.
- Everyone delights in telling you that whilst you were away they had a heatwave, but that torrential rain is forecast for the next six months

…But you don't care because *YOU'VE GOT A SUNTAN!*

HOW TO *REALLY* FLAUNT THAT TAN

- Wear white, black...or something really bright.
- Wear short sleeves and shorts...because you *can*!
- Try to keep putting your brown lean-looking arm next to pale clammy-looking arms of people at work.
- When anyone says you look very brown, say, 'Do you think so? I thought I was looking *really pale*'.
- Watch out for people sitting outside pubs with their skirts rolled up who are trying to catch a few rays...then walk right past them.

HOW YOU KNOW YOU'VE SUCCESSFULLY FLAUNTED

- People look for strap marks but can't find any.
- No one wants to sit next to you at work/school/on the bus.
- People only start being nice to you once you've started to peel.

Once you're home you nearly always have some regrets, like not seeing enough of the country, being such a sap about flying, not settling the score with the Family From Hell by superglueing their sunloungers

when they went for lunch, or forgetting to slip a copy of *Celibacy Can Be Fun* under the door of the couple next door. As you gradually get back into the routine of going to work and having to wear jumpers again, you turn to your toilet roll flamenco dancer and your photo album to bring back the memories of waking up to intense sunshine, feeling the bone-penetrating heat and having to wax your bikini line. The mirror is temporarily no longer your enemy, you look better in your clothes, you feel really glad you persevered and wore a bikini because you don't even mind looking at yourself in the bath, and for a few weeks at least you feel a bit of a sex goddess.

If you're lucky, the weather might be good enough to allow you to keep topping up the tan for the rest of the summer, but more often than not, the sun disappears the minute you land and you have to risk hypothermia in order to show it off. You'll probably still be in your shorts if there's a freak snowfall because, hey, you've got a suntan and are immune to the cold.

Well, that's just about it. You've prepared for, journeyed to and had your holiday. You've hopefully had a rest and enjoyed yourself and made all your friends sick at the sight of your skin. You've gone back to pushing the toilet handle down instead of pulling it up, got used to everything being back in sterling, and are once again waiting half an hour for a coffee and being spat at by waiters. You're coping with the trauma of going back to work when you'd much rather have stayed where you were forever, and have just about adjusted to normal life again...

...Either that, or you took one look at those sackfuls of washing and went straight back to the travel agents...